HER PERFECT MATCH

MISTRESS MATCHMAKER, BOOK 3

JESS MICHAELS

Her Perfect Match

Mistress Matchmaker Book 3

Copyright © Jesse Petersen, 2013

For more information, contact Jess Michaels

www.AuthorJessMichaels.com

To contact the author:

Email: Jess@AuthorJessMichaels.com

Twitter www.twitter.com/JessMichaelsbks

Facebook: www.facebook.com/JessMichaelsBks

Jess Michaels raffles a gift certificate EVERY month to members of her newsletter, so sign up on her website: http://www.authorjessmichaels.com/

*To Michael, for always understanding and supporting my weird quirks,
my mini-meltdowns and my dreams.*

CHAPTER 1

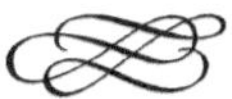

Vivien Manning spent her twenty-ninth birthday in the same manner as she had done the past three years. First, breakfast on the veranda of her London home overlooking the park. Then a morning of shopping with friends who had come bearing gifts which both delighted and surprised her. Finally, she capped off the day with a gathering she hosted each year to launch the Season. And now...well, now the time had come for her usual ending to the special day.

She looked across the room at the two naked men waiting for her on her bed. Two more different gentlemen there could not be. One was Trevor Smithing, the first footman of a friend who had bestowed him as her "gift" a few hours before. The very *handsome* first footman, probably eight years her junior with pale blue eyes and blond hair.

The other was Seymour Lawrence, tall, dark, with eyes the color of midnight. He was a wicked, wicked man, in more ways than one. A merchant who had worked his way up the ranks to riches beyond his wildest desire, he had been pursuing her for months and had finally agreed to this one-time tryst rather than a long-term arrangement.

Vivien shivered as she slipped her robe from her shoulders and presented her naked flesh to the men.

"Mmm," Lawrence purred as he stroked his hard, generous cock. "Even better than I imagined."

Vivien laughed as she moved toward the bed. Trevor stepped toward her, catching her in his arms when she was in reach and dragging her against him for a surprisingly passionate kiss. Vivien relaxed into the embrace. She'd been told tales of the sensual footman and his talents at pleasing ladies, and thus far his reputation lived up to its billing.

As he sucked her tongue and tasted every inch of her mouth, she felt hands come around her from behind. Lawrence stroked her hips with delicate caresses, even as he arched against her. When his tongue came out to trace her neck, she broke from Trevor's kiss with a gasp of breath.

"Shhh," the servant urged her as he cupped her face. "Just feel, Vivien. There is no need to do anything but feel."

She blinked as she stared at him. Once another man had said something similar. Another man on another night…

She shook her head. She was not about to ruin her birthday with thoughts of that. Instead she shut her eyes and returned her lips to his.

She drove the kiss this time, despite his reassurances that all she need do was feel. That wasn't her nature. It never had been. She took what she wanted and tonight she wanted to forget and to come.

Lawrence chuckled from behind her and glided his fingertips up her sides until he stroked her breasts. His hands cupped her, squeezing her flesh, tweaking her nipples between a thumb and forefinger. Her breath shortened and her knees went weak at the pleasure created by his touch coupled with Trevor's deep, erotic kiss.

"Now lie back," Trevor whispered as he nudged her toward the big bed. She'd had it designed specifically for pleasure. It was wider than the average bed and nearly filled the chamber. She took her place against the pillows as the men joined her, one on each side of her.

"Open your legs," Lawrence demanded, pressing a quick, hot kiss to her mouth.

She nodded and slid down a little, parting her legs to reveal a sex already slick and ready. Both men looked down her body with admiring expressions. She watched as they looked at each other, silent communication passing between them as to how to best take advantage of this brief and highly coveted night in her bed. After all, men fought over the right to be a part of her birthday pleasures.

This birthday, she had chosen exceedingly well.

In tandem, they slid down her body, Trevor moved slower as he glided his mouth over her collarbone, her chest, and finally settled at her breast, sucking one nipple between his lips and scraping his teeth over the already sensitive flesh.

Vivien gasped out her approval of this movement, but the gasp just as quickly turned to a moan as Lawrence reached her sex. He used his thumbs to spread her outer lips open and she jolted at the touch. But the feeling was nothing compared to when he brought his tongue down against her and began to lick her pussy.

She lifted her hips to match his rhythm as her head began to rock back and forth against the pillows. Pleasure circled, slow and steady around her body, focusing where each man took his turn in creating it.

But what Trevor was doing didn't seem enough for him. He glided lower, dragging his mouth down her stomach, her hip until he too lay just before the sex presented to him.

"Share?" he murmured.

Her eyes flew open as she watched the two men, lying close together, lock eyes. She shivered at the desire that coursed between them all, not limited to anything but pleasure. Lawrence nodded and moved over so that Trevor could take a place at her sex. The servant put his mouth where Lawrence had once been, while

Lawrence instead slid two fingers deep within her clenching sheath and began to pump inside her with gentle, building pressure.

"You're going to come," Lawrence told her, lifting his gaze to look at her.

"I most certainly am if you two continue like this," she gasped.

Lawrence had been most skilled at his oral pleasurings, but Trevor was a marvel. He was more driven to make her explode and focused his tongue right on her tingling clitoris. Added to Lawrence's ministrations deep within her body and she was ready to find release for what she hoped would be the first of many times this night.

It reached her in subtle waves, little burst of pleasure. She arched her back and moaned through it, but in truth the release wasn't as powerful as she had hoped it would be.

But then, that had been true of all her orgasms for some time.

She pursed her lips as the pleasure of her lovers' tongues and fingers slowed and ceased, then leaned up on her elbows to look at the men.

"Gentlemen, I would greatly like to feel you both inside of me."

Lawrence laughed, while Trevor's eyes went wide before he nodded.

"That is what I've always liked about you, Vivien," Lawrence said as he lay down on his back and dragged her across to straddle him. "You demand what you want."

Vivien smiled, but inside her stomach clenched. He was not lying, of course. She had built an entire empire around demanding and taking what she desired. But in her most secret heart, she often wished someone would give her what she needed without her being forced to take the lead.

Her thoughts were mercifully interrupted when Lawrence cupped the back of her head and dragged her down for another deep and passionate kiss. She pushed everything else away and shifted her position over his body. His hard cock nudged her entrance already, but she made no move to take him inside. She had all night for this pleasure.

Trevor watched them for a few moments, then he moved behind her with a moan of desire that seemed to reverberate through her even though he hadn't even touched her yet. When he did, that pleasure doubled, tripled. He knelt behind her and pressed two wetted fingers to her backside.

The jolt of sensation made Vivien's eyes go wide and she broke her mouth from Lawrence's to throw her head over her shoulders with a gasp of surprise and pleasure.

"Most excellent," Lawrence growled as he tugged her back to him. "Shall we begin?"

She met his wicked gaze with one of her own and then shifted, guiding his cock to her soaking entrance and taking him inside her. He was a large man, thick and long, and she eased herself into position, taking him inch by inch, wiggle by wiggle, until he was fully seated within her clenching, aching sheath.

She already felt impossibly full, but this first possession was only the beginning. Trevor's slow readying of her backside had continued all throughout her taking of Lawrence's cock and she peeked back at him to smile.

"Should I?" he asked, revealing a brief glimpse of the servant still living within him.

"By all means," she groaned as she lifted her ass slightly to allow him greater access. "I'm ready. Are you?"

Lawrence grinned up at her. "Very much ready to explode, oh yes."

She forced her body to relax, even though she pulsed with sexual tension, and then nodded to Trevor. He placed a warm hand on the bare small of her back and then pressed the head of his swollen cock to her bottom. The tight muscle of the rosette entryway gave way with gentle encouragement and he began to breach her in the most forbidden way.

Vivien gasped as the pain of the entry crossed into pleasure. She was so full she almost didn't know what to do or how to react. All she could do was feel these two men as Trevor buried himself and they all held still, panting together.

"Oh my God," the servant moaned from behind her. "I can feel everything."

Lawrence laughed and flexed his hips for a slow thrust that had both Trevor and Vivien moaning in time. And with that, slow was gone, thinking was gone, wonder was gone. The men began to take her, their rhythm matched so that as one cock slid away, the other drove forward. All Vivien could do was hold on as the pleasure built within her shaking body.

But even as that pleasure built, it remained muted. She squeezed her eyes shut, reaching for more, concentrating on the sensations with all her might. But although she could reach the edge of orgasm, nothing could push her over. Not the two cocks inside her, not the way Lawrence sucked her breasts as they made love, not the gasping groans of Trevor behind her.

Frustration built within her. Over the years, she had begun to resort to wilder sexual antics just so she could *feel* something. But there was only one thing that made her feel. Made her come. Made her wild.

But she couldn't think of that one thing. She refused. It was too dangerous.

And yet, as the pleasure stalled, she found herself picturing that one thing. That one man.

Benedict Greystone.

She saw him in her mind, leaning over her, pleasuring her, holding her and her body finally found release. She screamed as her orgasm tore through her from every side, rocking her hips out of control and milking each man with her spasms.

Neither of them could resist the pull of her strokes. Trevor withdrew first, the cream of his release spurting into his hand and across her sheets. With a few pounding thrusts, Lawrence followed suit, jerking free of her to spend between their sweaty bodies.

She flopped away from Lawrence to lie on her back against the pillows, her hand across her eyes. Her body still tingled, her limbs were heavy from pleasure, yet she silently cursed herself for what she had been driven to do to find that pleasure.

Benedict Greystone was not an appropriate subject of fantasy. He could not continue to make inroads into her dreams and her desire. There was nothing good to come of it.

"Was that an experience worthy of a birthday, Vivien?" Lawrence asked as he pressed a kiss to her throat and got to his feet.

She smiled up at him and at Trevor, who followed suit. She watched both men dress, marveling at how well built they each were, no matter how differently they were put together.

"Oh yes," she reassured them both. "Most fitting of a birthday. Thank you both for making it memorable."

Trevor finished dressing the fastest and gave her a quick bow. He had already returned to full servant mode.

"Miss Vivien, thank you again."

She nodded as he slipped from the room and left her alone with Lawrence. He looked down at her with a grin.

"A most proper exit for a man whose cock was just seated in your arse."

She laughed. "He did his duty and now he returns home. I'm certain his mistress won't allow him to sleep in just because he fucked me tonight, whether she encouraged it or not!"

"And what of me—do you wish me to leave you just as abruptly?" the other man asked.

She gazed up at him. He was uncommonly handsome, yes. Five years ago she might have allowed him to take the role of her protector, as he kept asking her to do.

But it wasn't five years ago. Or even three years ago. This was today and she was no longer the same person.

"Yes," she said with as kind a smile as she could muster. "We talked about this, Seymour. I am not seeking pleasure for more than a night at a time. You will find yourself a very fitting mistress. I can even assist you if you'd like. I'm known for that sort of thing, after all."

Lawrence grinned and shook his head. "You are determined to keep your independence, aren't you? I rather like that about you, my dear. Don't fret over me, I shall not demand you match me with someone else. And I will leave you now to your first morning of a new year. But do call on me if you change your mind."

He pressed a quick kiss to her cheek and departed the room, leaving Vivien alone. The first day of a new year of her life. A countdown to thirty, which seemed utterly ancient to her now.

And as she wrapped the sheets around herself, she had never felt so empty in her life.

CHAPTER 2

Light peeked through the gap in Vivien's curtain. She remained in her bed, though there was no rest to be found there. She had not slept since her visitors had departed a few hours before. She should have been sleeping in, luxuriating in the satisfaction of sin and pleasure.

Instead, she found herself restless and discontented, not by the pleasures of the night, but by her...*life*.

It was an odd feeling and she jerked herself out of bed to ring for her maid. As she pulled on a robe, she paced the room, trying to block out feelings that burned inside her.

How could she be dissatisfied? She had spent years, almost a decade, actually, building her life up to the standard she now kept. She had always taken pride in the vast fortune she had built and the reputation she had cultivated.

The door to her chamber opened and she turned to face the servant with a false smile.

"Good morning, Rachel. I believe I would like to start the day with a bath."

The young woman, her servant and companion for five years, stared at her as if she had sprouted a second head.

"What is it?" Vivien asked, perhaps a bit sharper than she should. "Why should you look at me in such a way?"

The girl scuttled into the adjoining room and rang the bell for hot water to be brought. "I'm sorry, Miss Vivien," she said with a shake of her head. "I only haven't ever known you to be up before seven before."

Vivien groaned. "Dear God, is it that early?"

"Yes, ma'am," Rachel said as she bustled for thick towels and soap. "It may take the staff a bit of time to ready the water. They won't be but just starting their day, you see."

Vivien moved into the room and sank into the lounge by the fire with a heavy sigh. She stared at Rachel.

"I hadn't thought," she said, apology thick in her voice. "There is no rush, I simply…couldn't sleep."

The girl turned toward her and there was concern in her dark eyes. "You have seemed…out of sorts lately."

Vivien flinched. She had very few people she confided in. Even her best friend Mariah and their newest friend Lysandra did not truly know all about her. No one did—she made sure of that fact. But outside of her friends, she *did* trust her servants. And she believed they truly cared for her.

After all, with what they saw, they all had ample opportunity to destroy her if they desired to do so. None ever had, even servants who had been dismissed from her employment over the years.

"Have I been out of sorts?" Vivien asked.

Perhaps if she hashed this out with another person, she might uncover the source of her recent melancholy.

The maid nodded. "Of course, no one else in the world would see it, ma'am. No one who comes to this house or sees you in public ever says anything except that you are the most beautiful and accomplished woman of your kind."

Vivien smiled, but inside her stomach clenched. *Her kind.* There was no doubt what that meant.

"But *you* can see something more," she said.

Rachel waited until the first set of servants had come with steaming-hot water. Once they had dumped it into the tub and departed to fetch more, she continued.

"Yes, I can. It seems you have been different since Miss Mariah… I mean, since Mrs. Rycroft's marriage."

Vivien pushed to her feet in shock. *Had* this out-of-sorts feeling truly begun almost a year ago? She would not have said it herself, but now that Rachel had, the date rang true.

"But I am exceedingly happy for Mariah," she whispered, more to herself than to Rachel.

She'd had a small hand in Mariah's match with her new husband, John Rycroft. Just as she had with Viscountess Lysandra Callis and her husband Andrew. Her reputation as a mistress matchmaker had been damaged by those two marriages in two years, but both women deserved their happiness. So she ignored the "Mistress Matchmaker turned Marriage Matchmaker" whispers and instead smiled at her friends and their intensely obvious joy.

"Of course you are!" Rachel insisted as the second set of water was poured into the tub. Now it was more than half full and steaming.

Once the men with buckets had gone, Vivien slipped from her robe and stepped into the water. Her aching muscles relaxed in the warmth and she settled back against the curved tub to stare up at the ceiling.

"And yet, I cannot deny that seeing not one but two of my matches end in *love* has made me—" She broke off, for the word on her tongue was *jealous*.

But that couldn't be correct. She had no desire for love or marriage or anything permanent. As Seymour Lawrence had said to her not five hours before, she valued her independence. She would not surrender that for something so fleeting.

"I'm tired," she whispered instead.

Rachel handed her the soap. "Oh, and why wouldn't you be? You hardly had any sleep. Perhaps the bath will help you relax and—"

"No," she said as she lathered the soap in her hands absently. "Not physically tired. Something deeper. I'm *tired* of being the most celebrated mistress in Society. I'm tired of hosting fetes and pleasure parties."

Rachel pursed her lips. "You have done so for so long. Who could blame you for feeling the shine has worn off the diamond?"

Vivien chuckled as she glanced up at her servant. The girl was very bright, really. "Yes. An apt metaphor."

"I suppose you could..." Rachel trailed off, her lips pursed in concern.

Vivien sat up straighter. "I could what?"

"Well..." Rachel glanced down at her. "You could...stop."

Vivien's lips parted. Dear God, she had never considered that. Being Vivien Manning, Courtesan Extraordinaire had become her everyday life. But what if it wasn't? What would she do if she was just...*herself?*

"I've spoken too plainly," Rachel fretted, wringing her hands in her lap. "I'm sorry, Miss Vivien."

Vivien glanced over at her. "No, no, Rachel, not at all. I asked you for your counsel and you have given that to me. In more ways than I could have imagined when I invited you up here to forget my feelings. But I think you may be...correct, though I cannot believe I am saying so."

Truly she could not, but when she said those words out loud, they gained even more power. She tingled with them, more excited by the idea of walking away from this life than she had been by any lover in...well, since her last protector.

"Correct?" Rachel whispered.

She nodded. "Having you say these things has made me realize I don't *want* to do this anymore. To be this person anymore. I—I want a new life. Where I can start over."

Rachel stepped back until she bumped the settee arm with her backside. Her voice trembled as she whispered, "Miss Vivien..."

"Oh, please don't look so forlorn!" Vivien burst out. "I could not just disappear in a moment's time. I wouldn't do that. I need time to arrange for a new home, a new name, to make sure my servants were taken care of. And have you ever known me not to make my exit spectacular?"

Rachel laughed. "No, miss. You have always sparkled on your way into any room and on your way out. No one could miss your entrances or exits."

"And this shall be no different." Vivien clapped her damp hands together as her mind raced. "If this Season is to be my last, I shall make it such a Season that when I disappear, my legend will be whispered of for years to come."

Her servant's eyes widened and then a grin began to spread across her pretty face. "Miss Vivien, that could be…"

"Extraordinary?" She laughed. "Oh yes. I very much intend it to be so. Now run into my dressing room and fetch a piece of paper and a quill. I have much to plan if this is to truly end my reign as Master of the Mistresses!"

The girl giggled as she rushed into the other room and brought back the items Vivien had required. Vivien sank back into the tub and pondered. Oh, there were many lists to be written. Things to do. Money to spend. Homes to find. Ways to remain anonymous in whatever new place she arrived in.

But right now she had an entirely different list on her mind.

"At the top of the paper, write 'Loose Ends to Tie Before Departing London'," she ordered as Rachel returned and took a place to write.

The scratch of the pen made her smile as she thought of everything she wanted to do to make this last Season oh-so-memorable.

"First, celebrate my friends." She sighed as she thought of them. She had many acquaintances and clinging hangers-on, but there were only a few people she counted as true friends. Mariah and Lysandra were chief amongst them. Before she vanished, she wanted them to know how much they were appreciated and loved.

"Yes, miss," Rachel said. "Second?"

"Destroy someone evil," she said with a frown. There were many she could count in that number. She had always remained silent to protect her reputation, but without those bonds? Oh, she could destroy. "And third, protect someone good."

"I like those," Rachel said as she scribbled away.

"I rather do myself. Fourth, indulge in pleasure." She hesitated. "I realize that may seem silly coming from me, since that is the life I intend to leave. But once I am a respectable woman with a new name, I do not think I shall have the freedom to carouse as I can do now. I shall have to get it all out of my system."

She glanced up to find Rachel blushing as she wrote down the item. But she was also smiling.

"Fifth?"

"Give away that which I do not need," Vivien said.

There was much that fit that description. She had amassed a great deal of wonderful things, some of which would come with her wherever she ended up, some would be sold. But if she could bestow some happiness from her things on to deserving parties, she wanted to do so.

"Sixth," she continued, "Enjoy London. For I do not think I will be able to return until age has changed my face enough to make me unrecognizable."

"Oh, Miss Vivien," Rachel sighed. "I do not like to think of that."

She shrugged, though in truth she didn't like to think of it either. London had been her home for ten years. It had given her wealth and solace after a painful childhood. She would miss it.

And yet, she did not feel a desire to alter her course.

"Number seven, I wish to revisit the past."

She hesitated as Rachel scratched out her sentence on the list. There were many things left unresolved in her past. Things that she dreaded facing. But she would. Once and for all.

"And while I am pursuing number seven," she said with false lightness. "I would also like to complete number eight and settle a debt."

"A debt?" Rachel said in surprise. "I beg your pardon, ma'am, I did not realize you were a gambler."

Vivien barked out a laugh. "Oh, all mistresses and courtesans are gamblers, my dear. But that isn't the kind of debt I mean."

No, she meant a debt to the man who had plucked her from a path of ruin and made her something more. She owed him something. She intended to repay that debt now.

"And finally, I suppose my final loose end will be to disappear," she said with a smile.

Rachel's hand faltered. "Disappear."

"Yes. That will lend the right twist to this grand gesture, I think. I shall vanish on the wind and leave the world gossiping."

Rachel slowly wrote her mistress's last loose end and then set the paper aside with a sad sigh. "Are you certain this is the course you wish to follow?"

Vivien hesitated. "I am not certain of much lately. I suppose that has been the cause of the malaise you have noticed. But of this course I am certain. And now, help me out."

Rachel moved to the edge of the tub with a towel in hand and helped Vivien step onto the floor. As she wrapped the towel around her mistress, Vivien sighed.

"I can dry myself. Go and finish whatever your normal morning routine is. I shall ring to be dressed in a few hours."

"Yes, miss," Rachel said with a quick curtsey.

"Oh, and Rachel?" she called out as the girl moved toward her door.

She turned back. "Yes?"

"I trust you, but I must ask you to be discreet. Please do not tell anyone, not even the other servants, of my plans. I will do so myself, when the time is right."

Rachel nodded. "Yes, miss. I will not speak a word of this. You may depend on me."

The girl slipped away. Once the door shut behind her, Vivien tucked the towel more firmly around her and moved to the list

Rachel had abandoned on the seat. In her neat handwriting, the girl had marked out a plan for Vivien's explosive departure from the life she had been living.

And when she looked at that list, she thrilled at its nine points. And realized there was one missing.

One loose end she had never resolved. One loose end that haunted her daily, weekly, monthly.

She caught up the pen, dipped it in ink and added a final number to the list:

10. *Benedict Greystone.*

Benedict Greystone lifted a slice of toast to his lips and took a bite as he scanned over the paper before him. Having dispatched with the business sections and important news, he had moved on to the large portion of the paper that dealt with Society and gossip. Most of the items were benign enough, a party here, a piece on the Regent and his estranged wife there.

But it was the blind items that often caught his eye. There, the writers sometimes made reference to people outside the normal social circles in circuitous descriptions one could easily decode if aware of the parties involved.

And there, the third item in, was the one he had been seeking, though he would deny it if asked.

A certain popular "lady" celebrated her birthday last night with a fete that would turn real ladies into vermillion-cheeked messes. The author wonders which of the gentlemen in attendance stayed after-hours to offer her a gift.

Benedict gripped the paper so hard that it crumpled and glared at the mess in his hands.

"Vivien," he murmured.

The woman was entirely inescapable. Not that he did a very good job of trying.

Behind him, he heard his brother clear his throat, though he had not heard Derek enter the room. He set the paper aside, but the Earl was already leaning over his shoulder glancing at what he had been reading.

"Vivien Manning?" his brother said with a cluck of his tongue. He took a seat at the head of the table next to Benedict and took the mangled paper. There was no masking his disapproval as he sighed, "Still?"

Benedict leaned back in his seat and shrugged. There was no use denying what Derek knew and had known for years.

"We cannot help who we love, my lord," he said softly. "Only what we do about it. And my duty is very clear."

Derek glanced at him with a brief flash of concern, but then he smiled. "Does this mean you will be taking my advice and begin a search for a bride, then?"

Benedict let his brother's question sink in and wished there would be a moment of excitement of pleasure at the thought. There was none. Only drudgery and duty and dread.

His brother turned the paper away from the Society page and Benedict let out a sigh. Now, at least, he no longer felt as if *she* were watching him.

"Yes," he finally responded. "It is time, I suppose. After all, you have married. As spare, I should be certain I too am doing my level best to protect the family name. The Earl requests it, does he not?"

His brother laughed. "Oh, please do not refer to me as if I'm not in the room."

"My apologies, I am merely still growing accustomed to your lofty title, brother," Benedict said with a smile of his own.

"Marriage is not as terrible as you make it sound with your tone," Derek reassured him, clapping a hand on his shoulder. "You should consult with Mother on the matter. I would wager she has suggestions for ladies who would be perfect for the job."

Benedict's smile fell and he paced away from his brother. "Oh, I'm certain she does. Horse-toothed heiresses abound, I imagine."

His brother folded his arms. "She chose my wife."

Benedict's heart sank at his brother's stiff posture. He had certainly put his foot in it this morning.

"Of course, I know that. And Jocelyn is beautiful both inside and out. You are lucky to have her as a bride and I am proud to call her my sister. I'm sorry."

Derek's countenance softened a fraction at Benedict's sincerity. He moved closer.

"You believe you love that Manning woman," he said softly. "But if you open your heart, you might find something similar with a woman of a proper class. A woman who would not use you."

Benedict gritted his teeth so that he would not tell Derek that Vivien had never used him. That would only cause a fresh argument on an old subject. Instead, he nodded.

"Perhaps you are correct that I will somehow stumble upon happiness in the ranks of the debutantes. You never know, stranger things have happened."

Derek hesitated and Benedict could see his brother had more to say. But he didn't. Instead, he glanced at his pocket watch and swore beneath his breath.

"I have an appointment I must leave for now. But we should talk about this again soon, Benedict." His brother clapped him on the shoulder as he passed by and out of the dining room.

Benedict sighed as he heard his brother depart and was left alone. Whatever his brother thought, whatever his mother said, the life that would greet him through their matchmaking was a very empty one.

And he was left feeling that none of it had meaning anymore.

CHAPTER 3

There was a mantra running through Vivien's head as she entered her ballroom a few days after her birthday.

Celebrate Friends, Celebrate Friends, Celebrate Friends.

She couldn't help but smile as she allowed the repetition to run over and over through her mind. It was one of the items on her unfinished business list. Once she had completed it, she would take the first step to her escape from London and the life she led here. The first step toward starting over.

It was certainly a most pleasant step to take, which is why she had begun here. She stared across the ballroom and found Lysandra and Mariah standing together with their husbands at their sides. Even though she felt a brief twinge of something a little unpleasant, she swallowed that back and instead enjoyed what she saw.

Lysandra had come to her two years before, a perfect stranger and an innocent one at that, begging for help. Vivien had arranged for her to be matched, albeit temporarily, with Viscount Andrew Callis and the two had fallen deeply in love. Vivien had been taken aback by the outcome. She had matched dozens of gentlemen with new mistresses over the years and had never seen one couple marry.

And then, just a year later, it had happened again. This time with

"

her best friend Mariah and John Rycroft. Although, to be fair, she had not exactly matched them. But she *had* encouraged their relationship.

But that fact mattered little. She had gone from being called the Mistress Matchmaker to the Mistress Marriage Matron almost overnight. And while most of that was teasing from friends, she *had* noticed fewer gentlemen asked her for help in finding a new mistress.

Still, she couldn't complain. Vivien had become close friends with Lysandra since the Viscountess wed and could see how truly happy the younger woman was. The match had been beneficial to her husband too. Andrew had gone from grief-stricken recluse to a man who laughed and loved.

The same was very much true for Mariah and John. In the end, she was happy for her friends.

Which was why she was hosting this fete tonight in celebration of their two unions. It was a far smaller gathering than most of her parties, without the sexual overtones hanging in the air. No, it was just a party amongst friends.

As she smiled, Lysandra caught her eye from across the room and moved toward her.

"*You* have a very odd expression on your face," her friend laughed as she slipped an arm around her waist.

Vivien returned the laughter even as she marveled at Lysandra's transformation over the past two years. She had gone from shy and frightened to a composed and confident lady. Love had done that for her.

"I do not mean to look *odd*, that is certain," Vivien said. "I was just pondering how happy I am for both you and Mariah, but also how your matches have lessened my requests from gentlemen to find new mistresses."

Lysandra shook her head. "Oh dear. I suppose many fear you will curse them with wives, not lovers. Heaven forbid."

Vivien shrugged. "It matters little. I did the service for one gentleman years ago and it somehow became a business of sorts. It was never something I asked to do. I shall not miss it."

She blinked as she looked around her once again. There *were* things she would miss when she was gone, though.

"This is a lovely party," Lysandra said, seemingly oblivious to Vivien's thoughts. "You were so kind to host it for us."

"Both of you have friends in our sphere," Vivien explained. "I realized I had been remiss in not celebrating your happiness with our friends. And I am happy to see such a good turnout when—"

She broke off and felt the blood drain from her face. Across the room, the crowd had parted slightly and she thought she had seen…

But no. It wasn't possible. Benedict Greystone had not been on the guest list tonight. She always checked those things carefully so she would never be taken off guard by his presence in her ballroom or anyone else's.

"Vivien?" Lysandra asked. "What were you saying?"

Vivien shook her head and opened her mouth to continue with her line of thought, but before she could, the crowd shifted a second time and her first thought was confirmed.

Benedict. In her home. Not ten feet away from her.

"I—why is Benedict Greystone here?" she whispered, unable to keep a slight crack from her voice.

Lysandra followed her line of sight and looked at him, then slowly turned her gaze back to Vivien. "I—er—*we* invited him."

Vivien blinked and tore her stare away from him to put it on her friend. "You did? But I did not see him on the guest list."

Lysandra shrugged, but her discomfort was evident.

"He is a friend of Andrew's, you know, from school. We saw him at the park yesterday afternoon and somehow the topic turned to this event. He seemed very interested in the subject, so we invited him."

Vivien said nothing. She tried not to look at him, but it was an impossible battle. She shot a side glance in his direction and her stomach fluttered. Dear God, but he was handsome. With dark hair, stormy gray eyes and broad shoulders, he always seemed to have stepped from the pages of a novel. A very naughty novel, as she considered all of his attributes when he was naked.

"I'm sorry," Lysandra continued, her voice dragging Vivien away from her thoughts. "I intended to tell you and it slipped my mind. I realize you two once...well, you were..."

Vivien arched a brow. Lysandra was still such an innocent.

"Lovers," she supplied.

"Yes. I should have told you. Is it horribly uncomfortable?"

Vivien swallowed. A loaded question if ever there was one. Was it uncomfortable to see the last man she had ever called protector? The one who she had shared such a passion with that it still resonated within her, no matter how she tried to forget him? The one who had told her he loved her? The one she had walked away from for so very many reasons.

"Of course not," she said with little strength to her voice. "Everyone knows that Benedict and I have stayed on very good terms over the years. I always enjoy seeing him."

Lysandra stared at her and Vivien could see she didn't truly believe her. Did that mean her conflicted emotions were obvious? That would not do.

"In fact, I should go and welcome him, since I did not do so earlier."

Lysandra nodded. "Would you like me to come with you?"

Vivien hesitated. There would be some comfort in having a buffer there when she spoke to Benedict. But he would know that was her reason for bringing her friend when she spoke to him. Showing him that weakness was not wise.

"I see Andrew eyeing you from across the room," she said with a motion toward the handsome Viscount. "You should join him and return your thoughts to those here to celebrate you. I'm perfectly capable of talking to Benedict on my own."

Lysandra smiled. "Of course."

Her friend stepped away and Vivien thrust her shoulders back as she began the short walk across the room to Benedict's side. She could do this. She had talked to him dozens of times since their parting. There was nothing different about this time.

Except that he was now her final item on a list of loose ends to resolve before she departed London forever. Only she wasn't certain she could ever truly resolve her complicated feelings for him.

Still, she smiled as she reached his side and prepared to pretend that his presence here meant nothing to her.

～

Benedict saw Vivien coming across the room in his direction from the moment she turned ever so slightly. But that was nothing new. Whenever they were in the same space, he couldn't help but be utterly aware of her and her every move. Her every breath. That was the curse of his feelings for her. They forced him to track her when he knew he should not.

His distraction must have been obvious, for the people he had been talking to a moment before moved off and left him alone as Vivien reached his side with a smile he knew too well. It was her false "mistress" expression meant to soothe and seduce. It wasn't real.

"Benedict," she said as she reached for his hands. She squeezed them briefly and then let them go, but the touch blasted him back in time to a night when they had lain out on the grass after making love, holding hands and staring up at the stars.

"Vivien," he managed to croak out. "This is a lovely party you have thrown together for your friends."

She tilted her head. "Yes. It isn't my usual kind of event, but I'm happy to celebrate all four of them and their marriages."

He swallowed back a biting word about her lack of desire for her own marriage and instead smiled. "Both the couples do look very happy."

She shifted ever so slightly and then rushed into a new topic.

"How have you been? I have not seen you in…it must be a few months."

Benedict pursed his lips. It had been four months, six days.

"Right after Christmas, I think it was," he said. "I returned to London to take care of some business and saw you at the opera, wasn't it?"

Her eyes widened when he could recount so many details, but he shook his head. If only she knew that he could recall even more. Like how her blonde hair had been styled in a different way that night. Like how she had smelled of lemons and rosewater. Like the exact cut and color of her blue gown.

He kept those details to himself. She had already rejected the idea that he would notice them. Rejected him. There was no changing that.

"I think you are correct," she said. "How have you been since then?"

"Very well," he replied, keeping up the same charade that she was. That they were acquaintances. "My family is well."

"Good." She remained smiling, but he could see the slight twitch in her cheek. Vivien had always known that his family did not approve of the relationship they'd shared.

Benedict clenched his hands at his sides. She had used that fact in her parting with him. Hidden behind their disapproval in a cowardly display when he knew there was more to her rejection of his heart. She had told him to move on with his life. And since that was what she wanted…

"I am being encouraged to marry," he said, watching her carefully for her response. "And I believe it may well be time for me to make that commitment."

She blinked. That was her only response. Just a flutter of her eyelids that betrayed she felt any deeper emotion about his announcement than she showed. It took her a moment to respond.

"I suppose it is time for you to pursue a new future." She hesitated as if she was going to say more, but didn't.

"Yes. A new future," he repeated, but there was no pleasure in the words he spoke. They felt like sand on his tongue.

She tilted her head. "You do not wish for this?"

He bit back surprise that she would be so direct. "You know what I wish for."

Now it was her turn to draw back. "Benedict—"

He waved his hand to silence her. "Please do not go through all your reasons for rejecting me. I have heard them all."

She was silent for a moment, watching him with a hooded gaze he could not read. Then she moved closer. "Benedict, it is true I cannot accept any future you have offered me. We both know why."

Except he didn't, but he said nothing and she continued.

"But I would be lying if I told you that I didn't still…think of you. Of us."

He stared. Was this happening? Was she truly saying these things after three years of polite distance and pretending to be friends?

"You do," he said, flat and emotionless for he feared revealing too much.

She nodded. "It seems there is unfinished business between us. On both sides. And since everything is about to change, I wonder if we should resolve that business, if only so it won't haunt us."

"What are you saying?" he asked softly.

She swallowed and her voice trembled as she whispered, "W-will you be with me again?"

He stared at her for he didn't know how long. This was like a dream. Or a nightmare he had lived out before.

Vivien shifted with discomfort. "Benedict?"

"I'm sorry," he said, shaking his head. "I'm certain I didn't understand you correctly. Will you repeat the question?"

Blood rushed to her cheeks, making them pink. He had so rarely seen her bashful that he stared at the sight.

"We have something still between us, Benedict. Before every-thing changes, I would like to resolve it. I want to be with you."

"Vivien," he whispered. "Why now?"

She was silent for so long that he thought she might not answer. Then she looked him in the eyes. "Why not?"

But as he stared into the blue depths of her gaze, he saw some-thing deep within that he thought she did not mean to share. A secret, a hesitation, something she was not saying.

And *fear* was there too. Fear which wasn't like her.

She reached out and squeezed his arm. He felt her touch crash though him like lightning and he almost recoiled from its power.

"Don't decide this very moment," she insisted. "I will wait for you tonight after the party. If you come to my room...you *come*." She emphasized the word so there was no doubt to its meaning. "If you don't...I understand and I will wish you nothing but the best."

She released him and stepped away. Without another word, she scurried into the crowd and left him standing, wrecked in her wake and totally uncertain of what he should do.

She offered him a return to the happiest time of his life. A sweet taste of passion and pleasure and all the love he still felt for her. But he knew that taste came at a cost. She had already made it very clear that they would never be together beyond an affair, beyond sex.

His brother had been telling him for years to walk away from Vivien. But he had never been able to do that.

And now might not be any different.

CHAPTER 4

"Y*ou* are distracted."

"What?" Vivien blinked, dragged back to the present moment as Mariah stepped up to her side and held out a glass of sherry for her.

Her friend laughed. "You see, your response proves my point exactly. I have been standing beside you for nearly a full minute and you didn't even notice me."

Vivien downed a sip of the drink. Her friend was right, but she wasn't about to admit it.

"Of course I noticed you!" she lied through clenched teeth.

Mariah arched a brow and it was clear she did not believe that statement even for a moment's time.

"Then why were you staring off into space, eyes glazed and in no way paying attention to your own party, even though your guests have slowly begun to depart? Is this some new technique to make yourself mysterious?"

Vivien rolled her eyes at her friend. "Very well, I *was* woolgathering. You would think that had become a capital offense to hear you grouse about it."

"No capital offense, I assure you. Simply something I am not accustomed to."

"I don't know why," Vivien protested. "No one can pay attention at all times."

Mariah shrugged as if conceding the point. "I suppose not, but you have always been the most attentive hostess. Which begs the question—what was on your mind that would so thoroughly change that?"

Vivien pressed her lips together so she wouldn't blurt out Benedict's name. Whatever was happening between them was a private matter and she didn't want her hawkish friends involved. Especially Mariah.

Of course, she didn't have to say his name at all. Her silence made Mariah shake her head.

"And what *was* the news from Mr. Benedict Greystone?"

"What do you mean?" Vivien asked, but her tone was weak even to her own ears. She would not convince anyone that Benedict wasn't on her mind with that waver to her voice.

Mariah set her drink aside, folded her arms and leaned closer. "I saw you talking to him a short time ago."

Vivien darted her gaze away from her friend. Her best recourse was to say nothing. Mariah knew she and Benedict had been lovers but little else beyond that. She might suspect something more remained between them, but she had no proof. And as long as Vivien stayed quiet, neither Mariah nor anyone else would see how many secrets Vivien had to keep. And how many plans there were to be talked out of if she dared speak of them.

"Well then," Mariah laughed when Vivien did not respond to her teasing. "Keep your council. I suppose you have earned your secrets and know very well how to keep them."

"It is my duty to do so," Vivien said with a false brightness her friend seemed to accept, for her expression changed from one of interest to one of warmth.

"Either way, thank you for tonight. I have missed being in the company of those you invited. I admit I was nervous to see old friends, but they have been very kind."

Vivien set aside her own troubles and thoughts and reached for her best friend's hands. She squeezed them gently. "You deserve *all* your current happiness and so much more."

Mariah's eyes swelled with sudden tears, but she shook her head.

"Don't sound so serious, Vivien! When you do it makes your words sound like it is an ending of some kind."

Vivien flinched. "I suppose it is," she admitted.

"It isn't." Mariah laughed. "I am only going home and I'll see you tomorrow for tea."

Vivien blinked. That twinge of guilt that had started in her earlier in the evening grew. She should tell Mariah her plans to leave London, to start over. And she would.

But not tonight.

"Of course," Vivien instead said with a laugh. "I will be at your house at three o'clock sharp."

Mariah leaned forward to kiss her cheek. As she leaned back, she looked at her closely and said, "Good night. Sleep well tonight. You need it, I think."

Vivien smiled as her friend moved toward her waiting husband and the door through the thinning crowd. Mariah meant well, but Vivien knew one thing for certain. There would be no sleep for her tonight, no matter what Benedict's decision about joining her might be.

Benedict stood in one of Vivien's parlors just outside her foyer and stared through the doorway as her party guests slowly maneuvered their way outside to their carriages with cries of farewell and orders to servants. Over half had gone home and still he debated with himself.

Should he leave and forget this night, with Vivien's bewitching offer, had happened? Or should he stay and open himself up to powerful passions and equally potent old wounds?

He gripped his hands at his sides and squeezed his eyes shut in frustration. His mind raced, but no matter how many options he considered, he could formulate no good answer to his questions. He was of two minds still—he *wanted* to stay, but he knew he *needed* to go for the sake of his sanity.

"Greystone?"

He opened his eyes and blood rushed to his cheeks when he found Viscount Andrew Callis, an old friend, standing before him, staring at him in concern.

"Are you well?"

Benedict considered the question and ultimately gave the polite response over the truth.

"Of course, very well," he said with a false grin that made his cheeks hurt. "Thank you again for including me in the invitation tonight. It has been an interesting evening."

An understatement if he had ever made one.

"I was happy we ran into you so that the invitation could be made." Andrew tilted his head slightly and examined Benedict closer. "Though I admit, I was a little surprised when you agreed to come."

Benedict tried not to show his reaction to the statement on his face and feared he failed. "Why wouldn't I? I am very happy for you and for Lysandra."

Andrew pursed his lips. "I appreciate that. Any friend we have in a higher social sphere is most welcome, considering the basis of our union. But I meant I was surprised given your history with Vivien."

"My history," Benedict repeated with a humorless bark of laughter. "Oh yes, I *thought* it was ancient history."

"Isn't it?" Andrew asked with lifted eyebrows. "It has been, what, two years since you two parted ways?"

"Three," Benedict corrected, his voice quiet. "Three years and nearly a month."

Images of the night Vivien rejected him flashed through his mind in rapid succession and he forced them back so they would not buckle him with renewed emotion.

Andrew's stare transformed from one of vague interest to concern with the specificity Benedict chose to use in his description. He leaned back on his heels and his appraising glance seemed to pierce through to Benedict's very soul. Benedict shook his head at the look. Damn it, but he was going too far.

For years he had successfully protected himself from the prying of others when it came to Vivien and his feelings for her. Only his brother knew the truth about the emotions that remained. But now, raw from her request, confused by his reaction to it, he could no longer seem to maintain control over himself.

"Is there something you wish to discuss?" Andrew asked, stepping closer to give them more privacy. "You seem very much ill at ease and I would like to help if I am able. I could promise you utmost discretion." He chuckled. "Even from my wife if need be."

Benedict turned on his heel and paced farther into the parlor. Andrew likely did not know how tempting an offer he presented. There was a large part of Benedict that wished to hash out his conflicted feelings and Andrew had always been a good friend when he needed one.

But once he said the things inside of him, they could never be taken back or pretended away again. And while he knew Andrew meant the offer of discretion when it came to Lysandra, if he betrayed that promise, there was no doubt that all of Benedict's words would come right back to Vivien. And the power they would give her...

It was too much.

"I trust your discretion, of course," he croaked past dry lips. "And I appreciate your offer of an ear. But at this point, I do not think I can explain what I do not understand myself."

He glanced over to see if Andrew would accept this mysterious explanation.

His friend continued to look concerned but said, "Very well. I would never demand a statement you didn't wish to share, of course. But I hope you know that if you need to talk, I am here in London for the remainder of the Season."

"Thank you," Benedict said, facing his friend straight on so that Andrew would know how much he meant his gratitude.

Andrew shrugged and stepped back. "Now I should go back to what I was doing, which was searching for my dear wife. It is late and I would much rather be at home in my bed than fighting the crowds through the London streets. Good evening."

Benedict nodded his goodbye and turned to face the low fire in the grate behind him. Though his emotions might remain conflicted, what he had to do was suddenly as clear as the freshly cleaned window across the room.

He had to leave.

If he couldn't control his emotions with a friendly acquaintance like Andrew Callis, then he had no chance with Vivien. And he already knew how sharing his emotions with her would turn out. He would be crushed. Rebutted. Rejected.

And that would not do. Not now. Not ever again.

He exited the room and passed through the crowd waiting for their carriages at the entryway to the house. His horse was tethered nearby and he didn't wait for a servant to fetch it. He released the animal himself, swung into the saddle and rode away.

But it was more difficult than it should have been not to look back in regret just one more time.

CHAPTER 5

Most nights, Vivien assumed she would be alone. Not for lack of offers from gentlemen, of course. Even tonight there had been a man who had leaned over and asked her to allow him to pleasure her. But more often than not she refused those who wished to add her as a mark to their manhood and accepted that a good book and a sherry were to be her companions for the night.

But tonight she *knew* she would be alone and it cut her to the bone.

Benedict had left her home three hours before. Without a word to her, not even goodbye. But his actions spoke volumes, didn't they? There was no refuting their meaning.

He didn't want her anymore. Or if he did, he wasn't willing to lower himself to her level to pursue that desire again. After all, hadn't he told her that he intended to seek a bride during this Season? Certainly running around with women such as her could do him no good on that score.

She sucked in her breath. Once Benedict wed, he would be faithful. That was the kind of man he was. Whatever they had shared would be truly over the moment he asked a lady to be his bride. He would forget her and devote himself to babies and country living with a woman of the proper station.

Her heart hurt at the thought, despite the fact that she had no right to her pain. She knew what she was. And in the past she had rejected Benedict's attempts to make what they shared more than a mere affair.

She paced her chamber for a moment, looking around the room restlessly. This wasn't the room where she took lovers and played the role of notorious mistress and courtesan. This was her *real* chamber. Where she could be Vivien. Only Vivien. Where she mulled her triumphs and her hurts.

Tonight was a hurt.

With a shake of her head, she moved to her dressing table and withdrew a slip of paper from the drawer. It was the list she and her servant had made a few days past. Her list of loose ends to tie up before she left the city and this life forever.

She sighed as she pored over each item. She had begun on the first item there. *Celebrate Friends.* Tonight had been a success, though it felt rather hollow at present. She still had a few things in mind, but she was well on her way to crossing this item off.

She scanned lower until she reached number ten. *Benedict.* She had rather hoped he would come to her, they would make love and that would settle her tormented thoughts about him. That she would end the night by crossing him off too.

Instead, she felt more ill at ease about the man than ever. But if he refused to join her in her bed, did that not resolve their loose end in some way? After all, his refusal of her offer did make it clear that he believed there was nothing left between them to discuss.

She reached for the pen on her dressing table and the corked bottle of ink beside it. Her hand hovered above the list as she prepared to cross his name off, even if the matter felt unfinished. But before she could do so, there was a knock on the door behind her.

She got to her feet. Rachel might have forgotten something

when she readied Vivien for bed. Smoothing her robe, she called out, "Come in."

She was surprised when her butler, Nettle, was the one behind the chamber door. He gave her an apologetic bow before he began to speak.

"I realize it is terribly late, Miss Vivien," he began.

She waved her hand. "Do not trouble yourself, Nettle, I wasn't abed yet. Is there something wrong? Something to discuss about the party tonight?"

She could scarcely believe it would be an issue regarding the party. Nettle had certainly seen far more scandalous ones without blinking an eye or commenting.

It was why she kept him in her employ. Trust and discretion.

"No, miss," he said with a darting glance in her direction that gave her pause. It was a look of concern and directed at her, though that wasn't Nettle's nature. "It isn't a problem with the household that brings me to your chamber. You have…a visitor."

All the breath left Vivien's lungs in that moment as she stared at the servant with wide eyes and shaking hands.

"A visitor?" she repeated on the barest of whispers. There could be only one person who would come to her now. "Benedict?"

The servant nodded slightly. "Yes, miss. Mr. Greystone has been shown to your…*other* chamber and awaits you there because I assumed that was still your desire. If I am wrong and you would like me to tell him that you are already abed and do not wish visitors, I will do so."

Vivien wrinkled her brow at the almost hopeful tone of the butler. Certainly Nettle had seen a great deal in his time with her, but he had never seemed offended by her late-night visitors. And he'd always seemed to especially like Benedict. When they were together, he had been far warmer with him than her other protectors.

"No," she insisted quickly, as if the man would dash from the room and send Benedict from her if she didn't hurry her response.

"I will see him. Tell him I'll join him in a moment. And you and the rest of the staff can take to your own beds. It has been a very long day for you, I'm certain."

Nettle hesitated, but then whatever personal thoughts he had been sharing with his meaningful glances and tone of voice vanished, leaving only her trusted servant in their wake.

"Yes, miss. I shall impart the message. Do ring if you have any need for anyone else tonight."

She nodded but didn't really notice as he stepped from her chamber and left her alone. She stared at her mirror again, but this time saw how bright her eyes and pink her cheeks were. She looked girlishly excited and she frowned.

This expression shared too much. She had to be what she always was: calm, collected, an experienced mistress. Benedict would expect no less of her. And she could be no more.

She covered her cheeks with cool hands to soothe them and drew a deep, calming breath.

"This is nothing," she reminded herself in a firm tone. "Just a tryst with an old lover, something you've done before without any consequence. This is just a way to cross Benedict from your list and move on with your life."

The words fell from her lips, her face calmed, but deep inside she did not believe or feel that coldness she expressed. With Benedict there had always been more than erotic connection. That was why she had broken with him, after all.

She turned from the mirror, turned from her thoughts and moved to the adjoining door. It connected to another plain chamber and through that was the room she shared with her lovers. She sucked in a breath, opened the door and skidded to a halt.

Benedict was standing across the room at the window, half turned toward what would have been a pretty view of her garden had it not been the middle of the night. He had already removed his jacket and draped it across the back of a chair near him. His cravat was also draped there. His dark hair was tousled, proof that he had been running his fingers through it during his wait for her arrival, and as he turned to face her, she saw that the first few buttons of his shirt had been undone.

Her knees began to shake, not because he was beautiful, which he had always been, but because coming into this room with him here waiting for her…it was like coming home.

A home she could not have. A home she had claimed she didn't want. And yet it slapped her in the face and stole all attempts she could make to be cool and collected in the face of his arrival.

It also stole her control. She had intended to speak to Benedict before anything else, but now she found herself crossing the room to him, her arms lifting around his neck like she did not control them, and then they were kissing.

His mouth was hot on hers, his lips tasted faintly of whiskey and his tongue felt like flame as it breached her and he claimed her with that touch. Her mind emptied, thoughts replaced by rushing blood and the sensation of her body readying for him. Already her nipples tingled beneath her thin night rail and her thighs were damp with desire.

"Vivien," he breathed between kisses, even as he backed her toward the big bed.

When her backside hit the edge, she sucked in a breath. Suddenly this was reality and she reveled in it after fantasizing over this very moment for so long.

But as she looked up at Benedict, she could not read his thoughts. His gaze, which had once been so open, was clouded, revealing only desire but nothing deeper. And even though it was better that way, she felt a twinge of regret that she could no longer see his love for her.

She swept the regret away and lifted her trembling fingers to his shirt. With a few movements, she had opened it and let her nails rake across the toned muscles of his belly. Both of them sucked in a breath at the sensation and Benedict dipped his head against his shoulders for a brief moment as she touched him.

She remembered every way he liked to be touched. It was burned on her like a brand and she leaned forward to press her lips to his chest. He groaned as she sucked one flat nipple between her lips and swirled her tongue around the disc. She felt his cock swell against her thigh and her breath grew short with excitement.

As she sucked and teased him, he went to work on the few items of clothing separating their bodies. Her robe was pushed away first. When he needed to push the fabric over her shoulders, it forced her from her attention to his body and she drew back, letting him glide the silky fabric away from her flesh.

He stared down at her, clad only in a nearly see-through night rail.

"Jesus," he breathed.

Pride swelled in her, unexpected and almost unrecognized it had been so long since she felt it when it came to her body. With most men, their compliments meant little to her, just empty words meant to seduce her.

This was something different.

She slipped her fingers beneath the thin straps of the gown and inched it down over her body to stand naked before him for the first time in over three years. Then she reached up, cupped his chin gently and brought him down for another kiss.

For a brief moment, he seemed almost too stunned to react, but when he did, it was explosive. He ground against her, lifting her onto the bed as he claimed her, punished her, explored her with the kiss. She hung on to him with both hands, fearing she'd be washed away by the strength of his growing passion.

He did not seem to fear such an outcome. He laid her down against the bed and joined her there as he parted her legs. He stared at her slick sex, open to him, ready for him, and for the first time he grinned.

She shivered, for she hadn't seen that look from him in years. It was wicked, possessive and filled with promise. Always when he looked at her in that manner, she ended up well pleasured and weak with release.

He leaned down and brushed his lips against her sex. She jolted with sensation and lifted herself toward him. His chuckle made her open her eyes and stare down at him.

She watched as he placed a hand on each hip and rolled her away so she was on her stomach. Now she only had a view of her headboard as he lifted her backside and faced her from behind.

She gripped her pillow with both hands and waited, waited for whatever he would do. He didn't keep her in suspense long. He buried his mouth against her sex from this new angle and began to drive his tongue inside her from behind.

She arched back, thrusting against him as her cries filled the quiet air. Pleasure built within her, powerful and intoxicating because she didn't have to work to achieve it. It came to her without effort, without frustration.

And when he reached around her body and pressed his thumb to her clitoris, the pleasure exploded into a starburst of release that pushed her body out of control. She cried out, she pressed back against him, her pussy jerked with spasm after never-ending spasm of pleasure.

He groaned against her entrance and the heat and vibration of the sound only increased her crisis. Then he pulled away, moved up behind her and glided his hard cock deep within her.

She gasped with renewed pleasure and surprise. She hadn't even realized he had freed his member from his trousers, but when she looked back over her shoulder, she saw that the black fabric drooped around his hips and he was buried to the hilt inside her.

She forgot reason and regret and everything else as he moved within her, forcing her through the end of her first orgasm and almost immediately toward another. They moved in tandem, slow and seductive at one point, fast and hard at another. They had no goal but mutual pleasure and enough experience with each other to reach that goal without exertion or struggle.

The second orgasm was less piercing than her first, but when it washed over her, it felt deeper, more persistent. She jerked her hips against the waves of it, gasping out Benedict's name as he continued his steady, forceful thrusts.

But as her sheath milked him with its orgasmic tremors, she could sense he was on the edge of control. Sweat glistened on his brow, his grunts and gasps were louder, and finally he growled out a sound of possession and she felt his hot seed splash inside her as he came.

They collapsed against the bed together, his body draped across her back with heavy, satisfying weight and she shut her eyes as she tried to pretend that this moment could last forever.

Benedict wasn't certain how long they lay together, their bodies tangled, their sweat and breath merging as they both came down from the ultimate high of mutual orgasm. All he knew was that he had been rocked to his very core by this act he had once feared he would never again share with Vivien. The act that had bound them for months before she severed their relationship in one quick sweep.

That thought lessened his pleasure and he rolled away from her to lie on his back in the gathering dark of the room. She followed his motion, resting her head against his chest. He wanted to distance himself, but how could he? It was as if his body had been sleeping since they parted and now he was wide awake and aware again.

He put his arms around her, tracing the willowy lines of her limbs absently.

She smiled up at him and his heart stuttered against his will.

"When you left here tonight, I admit I did not think you would come back," she whispered.

He didn't answer for a moment. Although they had just shared a deep passion, he didn't want to reveal too much of his feelings. He knew the cost.

"I wasn't going to," he admitted.

She lifted her head and looked at him in surprise. "No? Why did you, then?"

He cupped her face. Her skin was like silk against his fingers and the way her eyelids fluttered at his touch stole all his ability to protect himself.

"You know why," he whispered.

Surprise was the first emotion that washed over her face, followed swiftly by the same fear that had always accompanied any declaration he'd ever made that could be construed as emotional. But there was also something else there, lingering in her eyes—sadness. As if what he said made her ponder some great loss.

"Benedict—" she began and her tone was as familiar as her touch.

He pushed away and got to his feet. "We both know what I want from you isn't possible. I have accepted that fact."

He dared to look at her, but was surprised that there was no relief on her face when he said those words. In fact, her emotions, which had been so clear a moment ago, were now hidden. And yet she was still glorious. She had sat up when he left her and the sheets barely covered her. In the dying firelight she looked like a queen.

Renewed need pinched at him, melted him even when he didn't want it to be there.

"Do you still want me?" he asked, his tone carefully neutral.

She nodded without hesitation. "I...do. I think I made that perfectly clear tonight."

"Then perhaps I will come to you again," he said, making the words a statement rather than a question. He didn't want to give her the power in this decision, even though in truth, she had it all.

She hesitated for a moment and then nodded. "Yes."

He blinked. Yes? Had she actually agreed to see him again when it seemed like yesterday that she had sent him away, never to touch her again? Wild joy sprang up in him, but he pushed it aside.

He approached her with as much nonchalance as he could and bent to kiss her one last time. She tasted like strawberries, like honey, like passion, and he drank in all her flavors as the kiss spiraled into lust in a heartbeat. Finally he managed to pull away. He was too emotional to continue this tonight.

He stepped away. "Then I will see you again, Vivien. Good night."

He turned to the door without waiting for her to respond, though he heard her faint goodbye as he shut the chamber door behind him. He moved down the hallway and out into the night, but every step was made from instinct and memory, not because he was paying attention.

At that moment, all he could think about was Vivien. Tonight he had been utterly satisfied in a way he had not felt since the last time he left her bed three years before. But he was also completely confused. And wholly uncertain if the path he had just set himself on was one that would bring him joy or crushing heartbreak.

CHAPTER 6

Vivien turned to the next aisle in Mattigan's Bookshop and breathed in the scent of leather book covers and thick paper pages with a sigh of pleasure. This trip out was just what she needed to forget the past few days' events.

Since the night they'd made love, Vivien had received no word from Benedict. She hated to admit it, but she found his silence odd. During their affair three years before, she had become accustomed to his habit of sending her a note each day, even if they were not scheduled to meet. In truth, she had kept all the correspondence from him, from the banal to the passionate, in her *real* chambers, though she hadn't dared look at them since they had parted.

But this time, he seemed less interested in maintaining a relationship with her. His silence revealed that fact.

It was for the best, of course. She only wished to tie off the loose ends that remained between them, not become his lover again. Certainly, she did not wish to intertwine their lives in any way. Still, it stung when she allowed herself to examine the bare facts of his rejection.

She shook her head and turned her attention back to the books before her. The sixth item on her unfinished business list was to enjoy London and finally she was pursuing that endeavor. There was no use muddying its pleasure by thinking of a man who only confused her.

But dear God, he was all she *had* thought of since his departure the night of her party. Every time her bell rang, she lurched with anticipation. When she saw a man on the street with his build, she went weak in the knees. She heard his voice in crowds and in her parlors.

Even now she thought she caught the echo of it on the breeze as a new customer entered the shop.

"And a good morning, Mr. Greystone," the proprietor of the shop called out toward the door in reply to what the voice in her head had said.

Vivien froze. Well, this was certainly a most interesting development to her imaginings, hearing his name on the wind. That or Benedict truly was on the other side of the bookshelves.

She crept to the end of the aisle and glanced around toward the entrance to the street. There, as real as any other person in the shop, was Benedict. He leaned over the wooden countertop beside the door, talking to the shop owner with a nonchalance she hadn't seen in years.

"So, Mattigan, have my orders come in yet?" Benedict asked.

The shopkeeper smiled broadly. "Two of them, yes. The other three did not come in this shipment."

Benedict's expression fell a fraction, but then he shrugged. "Ah, well, it only gives me an excuse to peruse your shelves yet another week."

"I will fetch your selections from the back while you do so, sir."

"Very good," Benedict said, then turned on his heel and headed straight for Vivien's own position in the store. She scurried back into the aisle and clutched her books against her chest. He was coming directly for her and in her panic she had no idea how to handle the situation.

Pretend coolness? Act as if she did not see him? Run for her carriage like a banshee?

She squeezed her eyes shut. "You are being foolish," she admonished herself in as stern a tone as she would use with a wayward servant.

Thrusting back her shoulders, she moved toward the end of the aisle just as Benedict came around the corner. He was looking at the shelves of books intently and for a moment she was caught up in the sight of him.

His hair was slightly tousled from the windy day and he lifted one strong hand to smooth it as he continued to look at the books. His gray eyes darted from one title to another, entirely focused on what was before him. Sort of like when he had her in bed.

She blinked. He was looking so intently at the books that she could easily slip away without being noticed. But she wasn't going to do that. If she did, she would surely curse herself for days.

Instead, she moved toward him and cleared her throat to catch his attention. "Benedict, er, Mr. Greystone."

He lifted his head and slowly turned to look at her. His bright eyes were wide with surprise and his mouth tilted up in a grin she didn't expect after his avoidance of her.

"Great God, Vivien…Miss Manning. I didn't expect to see you here today."

She tilted her head. "Nor I you. When I heard your voice, I thought I was dreaming."

He arched a brow. "Do you often dream of me in bookstores?"

She laughed even though the question was a loaded one. "You must know you are dreamed of by dozens of women. I could not say I wasn't one of them."

The smile remained on his face but left his eyes at her response. Abruptly, he returned his attention to the books.

"And what are you doing out and about today?"

She hesitated. She had kept her ultimate goals secret from her best friends. She couldn't tell Benedict. Especially not Benedict.

"Vivien?" he asked when she pondered the question too long.

"I am enjoying London," she blurted out, quoting directly from her list. "I fear I do little of that, even though I have lived in the city for nearly a decade."

He glanced at her, appraising. "A lofty goal—there is much to enjoy. And Mattigan's is as good a place to start as any. Though you must know that, with your love of books."

Vivien shifted. Despite everything, he did know her well. Better than any other lover she'd ever had. "I have never been before today, actually."

He swiveled to face her directly, his face a mask of disbelief that made her very uncomfortable. She was accustomed to ruling her own world, but when she left its borders, she was often ill at ease.

"You needn't look at me like that, Benedict," she snapped, forgetting propriety in this public sphere. "You must not be as shocked as you pretend. A woman such as myself doesn't belong in a shop where the Prince himself sometimes buys his books. I have no place in museums and parks and all the places where dignified people congregate. Even you, who claimed to care for me beyond my station in life, didn't parade me out with the upper class. You kept me where I belonged, the opera house, the ballrooms of your closest friends and the bedrooms of my home."

He flinched as if she had slapped him. "Great God, Vivien, I had no idea you felt this way."

She turned her face. She did sound very bitter when she said those words to him. Was she bitter? She had never felt that way until now…

He moved toward her and his hand fluttered as if he wanted to reach out to comfort her. Embarrassment, uncommon and unwanted, filled her and she backed a step away to avoid increasing it further with his touch.

"You are a lady of the highest order," he said softly. "Whatever your 'station' in life, it does not change that. You belong in this shop, as well as any other place in London you desire to travel."

She shifted at his kindness and the sudden focus of his stare, then shrugged them both off.

"It is a good thing, then, for I intend to go to all of them before —" She broke off. There was no need to say anything more. "It doesn't matter. I heard you say to the shopkeep that you had books on order."

His concern remained on his face as he answered her. "Yes. I come in once a week, on this day, when Mr. Mattigan receives his newest shipments. I check on my orders and browse the new arrivals."

"Mr. Mattigan?" She blinked. "But this shop has been here for two hundred years. Don't tell me that a Mattigan still runs the place."

"Oh yes." Benedict nodded as if the statement were as solemn as a prayer. "He and his father and his father's fathers have served our city for years. That is why their reputation is so great."

Once again, Vivien felt uncomfortable in her very skin but pretended it away.

"And I see you have not resisted their lure either." He motioned toward her books. "Might I look at your selections?"

She hesitated and clutched her books closer out of habit. She had often felt that the books one read were a peek into the soul of the reader. That was why her personal library was kept in a locked room very separate from the places where her visitors went for her wild parties. Sharing these selections with Benedict felt so very intimate.

"Of course, you are not obligated," he said softly and began to withdraw his waiting hand.

She thrust the small stack toward him. "Certainly, you may look. As long as you promise not to take what I've chosen for your own."

He laughed, but his face was unreadable as he looked at her titles. "Ah, a collection from Sir Walter Scott. Very nice, I've always liked his poetry. *Sense and Sensibility*, but surely you have read this one."

She nodded after a moment. "Y-Yes. It is one of my favorites. I only rather liked this binding."

He held his gaze on her for a moment and then nodded. "And finally, *Gulliver's Travels*." He blinked in disbelief. "Truly?"

She laughed. In truth, she had chosen the last book because it involved such a grand adventure that she felt, in some small way, it mimicked her own future.

"It was something different," she lied.

He shrugged as he handed the books back to her. "And where will you go after this?"

"I think the British Museum," she said, thinking of no reason to lie.

"Oh excellent, they have a newer exhibit there of some of the Roman sculptures. I have been aching to find time to see it," he said with a clap of his hands. "I'm sure you'll like it."

She remained silent. Once again, she felt her ignorance and lack of experience in a way she was not accustomed to. When she didn't respond, he stepped closer.

"You *have* been there, haven't you?"

She swallowed. "No."

"Great God, no? With your sensibilities?"

A shrug was all she could manage to maintain the illusion of distance. "As I said before, these weren't exactly places I belonged."

"Poppycock!" he burst out. "The Museum is a place for anyone of intelligence and that is most definitely you. But perhaps—"

He broke off and she stared at him. "Perhaps?"

He cleared his throat. "Perhaps you will allow me to be your escort, since you have never had the pleasure of the place and I am a frequent visitor."

Vivien worried her lip. Enjoying London was one item on her list…Benedict was another. Spending a day with him *could* allow her to cross off two things at once. But merging him with the rest of her list…putting him too near the truth…it seemed rather *dangerous*.

And thrilling. And irresistible, despite the negatives.

"I would like a more experienced guide, but only if it will not disturb your own plans," she said softly.

"Not at all," he said with a wave of his hand. "Anything else on my agenda can be altered with ease. Why don't you make your purchases and I will send your driver on his way. We'll take my carriage."

She looked toward the exit of the bookshop. "What about your purchases?"

"I'm certain Mattigan has already put them on my account and handed them over to my servant." He shrugged. "So all that is left to worry over is you. I will see you outside?"

She nodded blankly and watched him curve around the end of the bookshelves. She heard him call a quick farewell to Mr. Mattigan, then the bell on the door jingled as he went outside to make arrangements and wait for her.

Slowly, she made her way to the counter to pay for her books, but each step felt as though it were out of a dream. How in the world had she been so utterly swept away in the middle of a bookstore?

And why didn't she care, even though she knew the consequences could be devastating?

Benedict had lied about a great many things in his life. His latest lie was that he had nothing better to do on this day than take Vivien for a tour of London. In truth, he had several meetings scheduled, both with family and business associates. Ones he feared he would pay for missing.

But at that moment, sitting in his carriage across from Vivien, heading to one of his favorite escapes in London, he did not care. All the questions and frustration he would surely encounter tomorrow were worth it.

Vivien tucked a stray lock of blonde hair that had escaped her bun behind her ear. As her bright blue eyes darted from one part of the carriage to the next, he saw her pale with recognition.

"It's been a long time since you rode in this rig," he drawled.

She nodded, lifting her fingers to trace the fine leather seat beside her, then the shining mahogany wood trim near the window. "Yes," she admitted. "I am surprised you still have it, let alone still drive it."

Benedict pursed his lips. He had kept the thing for...well, a great many reasons. But he hadn't taken it out for years, not until the night they last made love. Then suddenly he wanted to use this carriage.

"I keep it for its sentimental value," he said, his voice harder. "It was the last place we made love before you ended our previous affair."

She jerked her gaze to his and when he held it unflinchingly, she looked away. An uncommon blush darkened her cheeks. "But I suppose it is not the last place we made love anymore."

He tilted his head. "I suppose not. Do you think I should sell it, then?"

She didn't look at him. "It is hopelessly out of date. Why keep something like this just to cling to the past?"

He shook his head. "I don't know, Vivien. I ask myself that about a great many things. And yet I keep them."

She glanced up and he could see how uncomfortable this conversation made her. Good. He had spent years feeling uncomfortable, angry, sad, broken...a great many unpleasant things. Let her have her share in them too.

"Living in the past isn't right. It keeps us from our future," she said softly.

Now it was his turn to shift with discomfort. They had turned from the benign topic of a carriage long ago and now that they were dancing around something deeper, he wasn't sure how to proceed. In truth, Vivien had never allowed him to see much past her exterior. When he had, it had taken a great deal of work.

And why bother to do all that work when he knew in the end he still would not have what he desired most?

"Wise advice," he said and turned to look out the window.

To his great relief, the large façade of Montagu House rose up before him, signaling the end to the carriage ride. As the driver stopped, Benedict said, "The Montagu family sold this place to the Crown for twenty thousand pounds over fifty years ago as a location for the museum."

Vivien looked out as the door was opened by the footman. "It must have been nice to have an extra London estate just lying about to sell off."

He laughed with her while she stepped onto the drive and looked up at the pretty former home. It was done in a classic style with vast gardens stretching out on the stroll before the entrance.

"Oh, it is beautiful," she breathed. "I've always thought so, every time I've driven by."

"Wait until you are inside," he said, stepping out onto the drive beside her. "The wonders within are amazing."

So often Vivien only displayed what Benedict had always called her "mistress face" around others. It was an expression of false brightness, of distant indulgence used to place herself away from her companion. But now as she practically vibrated with excitement, he felt he was with the *real* Vivien. That had happened a handful of times during their previous affair, and he had longed for those moments since.

But they had always been brief glimpses into the real woman Vivien was. When she realized she had given too much of herself, she always stepped away. He'd often wondered if that was the real reason they had parted ways: that Vivien feared he was getting too close to her true spirit.

He all but held his breath as he waited for her to force that façade back into place. Or to leave his side just so he would no longer see her girlish delight at the museum and the contents that awaited them.

Instead, she slipped her hand into the crook of his elbow and looked up at him with those same shining eyes and wide, real smile.

"I cannot wait another moment to see everything—shall we go in?"

For a moment, he couldn't breathe, couldn't think, couldn't move as he stared into her eyes and saw so much beauty, so much truth...but then he shook his head and led her into the museum. This was a rare opportunity. He refused to miss a moment of it while he pondered what he had done to deserve it.

CHAPTER 7

Vivien clasped her hands together as the carriage jolted away from the British Museum three hours after their arrival. The late-afternoon sunshine streamed through the vehicle windows as she leaned closer to Benedict.

"And the Roman statues!" she gasped, continuing a line of conversation she had begun the moment they stepped from the museum onto the drive. "They are magnificent. When the gallery is fully finished, it will truly be a sight to see. The Venus was especially beautiful and—"

She broke off as a slow smile spread across Benedict's face.

"I am rambling, aren't I?" she asked as blood warmed her cheeks. "I have been going on and on for ten minutes and you have not had a word in edgewise."

"I like it," he said with a laugh that seemed to rumble through her body and into her very soul. "I don't think I've ever seen you so animated before. You truly enjoyed yourself."

She dipped her head. All day she had been too truthful, too open, but she couldn't help it. This was like a moment stolen from time and she had chosen to enjoy it rather than distance herself from it.

"I did," she admitted. "I cannot believe I've never gone before."

"I hope you will go again," he said softly. "There is talk they're going to build a newer, larger complex to house all the exhibits and collections. It will be a few years before it comes to fruition, but that should be a great sight to see, as well."

Vivien pursed her lips. This summer there would likely not be enough time for her to go to the museum again. And by the time a new and glorious complex was built, she would be long gone and forgotten.

Even by Benedict.

She smiled and felt the mask of the role she'd played for so long slide effortlessly into place. "For now, I fear my only destination shall be home."

He arched a brow. "So the bookshop and the museum are all you will do on your quest to enjoy London?"

She shook her head at his teasing, taunting tone. "It would be impossible to do everything and *see* everything in London in a day. I would be a fool, a very tired fool, to try."

He lifted one shoulder. "Perhaps you are correct. But I have one more suggestion of an experience to end your day. *If* you will trust me."

Vivien stared at him. He had a half-smile on his face that made him look more boyishly handsome than ever. He was teasing, but the choice of his words made her stomach tense. Trust was a commodity hard to come by, even with Benedict.

Still, she found she didn't want this day to end. Slowly, she nodded. "Very well. What do you have in mind?"

"A secret," he laughed. "You'll see soon enough."

She glanced out the carriage window to find they had turned away from the main areas of London, away from her home, and were now heading into the parts of the city where buildings were smaller and more spread apart.

"What if I had refused your request?" she said with a shake of her head.

He laughed. "Then I would have had my carriage turned around, of course."

She folded her arms with a smile she couldn't help. "You are always so certain of yourself."

His smile faded slightly. "Never with you. You forever set me off my axis."

He inched closer and suddenly there was a tension in the carriage that had nothing to do with teasing flirtation or friendly discussion. He wanted her.

And Vivien wanted him equally.

She leaned forward and whispered, "Should I apologize for affecting you so?"

He shook his head slowly. "No. I *like* being off-kilter."

"Good," she said as she moved to the seat next to him and leaned up for a kiss. "Because it's devilishly fun to set you that way."

His lips brushed hers and all her words vanished in an instant, replaced by sensation so powerful that her knees went liquid and her heart raced to an alarming rate.

He glided his arms around her, cradling her in an embrace that was gentle, emotional and yet possessive at the same time. She felt his passion for her, but also a shadow of those deeper feelings he had once confessed to her. His love.

That word had sent her flying away from him once. And it was something she could not face today any more than she could three years before, especially since she intended to leave London forever by the end of a span of a few short months.

But she didn't want to pull away from him. She *wanted* to feel his strength and his desire and his warmth. She wanted to be close to him…just not so close that either of them would get hurt. Right now this moment was so charged, she could scarcely think of what could allow her both desires.

She drew back, ready to distance herself, and suddenly it became clear. With a wicked smile, she placed her hand on the hard, thrusting outline of his cock, pressing the front of his trousers in a wild demand to be freed and inside her. He grunted out pleasure and rested his head back against the carriage seat as she began to rub him through the cloth.

He reached for her, but she dodged his silent demand and continued her torture a moment more before she began to unfasten his breeches. His member bobbed free and she looked down at him.

She had been with many lovers, but she had always been most impressed with Benedict's cock. Some men reveled in their girth and length, believing that those facts alone were what pleased a woman. Benedict had both in abundance and yet always worked to find the right stroke, touch the right place, use that tool for the best ends possible.

She stroked down over him, skin on skin now that his breeches were no longer in the way and he let out a garbled sound of pleasure and surprise as he reached for her once again.

Dodging a second time, she laughed. "No, no. You do not direct me, Benedict. You should recall that if nothing else."

His eyes lit up with challenge and for a brief moment, Vivien wondered if she had made a mistake by awakening his contrary side. But then she refocused on matters at…or *in*…hand and leaned over his cock.

"I am going to take what I want now, Mr. Greystone," she said, letting her hot breath gust over his sensitive flesh. "And you are going to enjoy it."

He opened his mouth to say something, but she dropped her mouth over his cock and instead of words, only a long, garbled moan escaped his lips. He settled back against the seat and surrendered.

She smiled against him and he hissed at the movement. But the hiss disappeared when she began to stroke over him. Even after three years and intervening lovers, she remembered each movement he liked best. She swirled her tongue around him in a slow, clockwise circle, then reversed the movement until he gripped at the carriage seat with both hands. She glided him into her mouth until the head of his cock bumped the back of her throat, then retreated until he nearly left her mouth entirely.

And she did all these things in slow, smooth motion, torturing him with the pleasure, reminding him that in this, at least, she could take control.

He growled her name and dug his fingers into her hair in an animal display of passion, gently forcing her to change her rhythm. Vivien groaned against him and it wasn't for show. Benedict was a sensible man, not prone to outbursts of violence or domination, but in the bedroom, when he made demands, it aroused her beyond reason. Even now, her pussy twitched as he guided her head up and down over him in a fast, rough rhythm. She found herself lost in it and stroked him with her hand as well as her tongue as the passion built, his control weakened and finally, with a shout, he came.

She took every drop of his sweet essence, milking him through the crisis until he went limp in her hand and equally limp against the seat. Looking up at him from his wet, spent cock, she smiled.

"It has been a long time since I did that with such pleasure," she whispered.

He grinned at her, the unmistakably triumphant expression of a highly satisfied gentleman.

"Equally long since I felt such release, I would wager," he laughed, then reached down to fix his appearance. "But I owe you an equally powerful release now. And I very much look forward to returning that favor."

She blinked. "I do not keep count of such things, Benedict. I did not pleasure you because I desired you to owe me a boon. I did so because I wanted to perform the act."

He tilted his head. "And I wish to do the same for you. Do not make our new…*relationship*…more complex than it must be, Vivien."

Vivien tilted her head. The way he emphasized the word "relationship" was quite dismissive, as was his expression as he finished tucking himself back in and refastening his buttons and hooks.

Perhaps she had read his intentions wrong. Perhaps this time he felt no bond to her other than a desire to have her in his bed.

Which was a good thing. Only it felt less than pleasant.

But she did not get a chance to brood over this new development overly long, for the carriage began to slow as it turned and then came to a stop. She pushed the curtain aside and outside was a large, beautiful park she had never seen before. Just a few feet away from the street was a magnificent lake with a blanket spread out on its shores and covered with a spread fit for the Queen herself.

The door opened and a footman reached inside to help her out. She took his hand without breaking her gaze from the pretty scene ahead of her. As Benedict stepped down beside her, she turned to him.

"Tell me that this isn't for us," she gasped.

He grinned. "I can tell you that, but it will be a lie."

She gaped as she looked again. Somehow, in the span of a few hours, he had arranged this. For her. A gift she hadn't expected, but now that it had been given, it touched her heart.

The one place she could not share. Especially with him.

As Vivien stepped toward the picnic his staff had arranged for them, Benedict could see her surprise written on every line of her face. He rather enjoyed seeing it in one sense. Vivien often covered her reactions, so seeing them was a rare treat.

But in another way, he was troubled by her surprise and shock at the arrangements he had made. Did no one think to do something nice for her anymore? Was she so alone and isolated from any affection that it took her so off guard?

She moved toward the picnic blanket as the carriage moved away to offer them privacy. But she didn't stop there—she continued strolling over to the lake and stared at the water, her eyes clouded with thoughts he wished she would share.

"Does this not please you?" he asked as he moved to stand beside her.

She jolted, almost as if she had forgotten he was there. "Oh no, on the contrary, it is lovely," she reassured him. "I was just thinking—"

She broke off and he frowned. That was the one constant—Vivien did not give of herself in any way beyond her body.

She looked off toward the road in the distance and shifted. "You know my family home is just a few hours outside town in the same direction we were traveling to come here," she mused, so quiet that it was obvious she spoke more to herself than to him.

He drew back in surprise. She had never spoken of her family to him, not in all the months they had shared a bed and a life together.

"Where would that place them?" he asked, cautious for fear he would frighten her away if he pressed too hard.

She continued to stare off toward the road. "A tiny little village called Sapsgate."

He frowned. He'd never heard of the place and he wished he had. He wished he'd traveled through there dozens of times, if only to make some kind of connection to the person Vivien had been before she came to London and closed herself off for her role as mistress of mistresses.

"When I came to London, I recall passing by this park. Perhaps we even stopped here to take our ease before continuing on to the city," she whispered, still lost in memories he could not access.

"How old were you?" he asked.

"Eighteen," she said, then shook her head as if she was just remembering where she was and who she was with. She smiled at him.

He balked. He knew a little about her history, the parts that were public. She had taken her first lover ten years ago, becoming an instant point of interest from the moment she stepped into Society on the arm of...who had it been? He could not recall.

"You very quickly came into the life of a mistress," he said. "You were nineteen when you became well-known."

She shrugged off the statement and moved toward the blanket to look at the spread before them. "My goodness, Benedict, your cook looks to be as spectacular as ever if this food is any indication! Is it still Mrs. Sterling?"

He drew back a fraction. "I'm shocked you remember that! Yes, she is still with me."

Vivien dropped to her knees on the blanket and spread her skirts around her for more comfort. She took an olive from a crockery container and popped it between her lips.

"It is my duty to recall a great many details about the men in my life."

He sat down beside her and watched as she began to load a plate with all his favorites from the selections before her.

"Do you mean to tell me you recall the names of every cook from any lover you've taken?" he asked as he took the plate she offered. "As well as every lover's favorite dishes?"

She smiled. "Your favorite dishes may be the only ones I recall, I admit."

Benedict straightened up at that unexpected admission and her face faltered slightly before she pushed forward, talking to fill the space.

"And Mrs. Sterling was a stunning cook. Of course I would remember her. I suppose there are little details I recall about any man with whom I spent significant time. It is the nature of my role to notice details and retain them."

Once again, she shrugged off any connection that remained between them as a symptom of what she did, what she *was*. But Benedict had seen the twinkle in her eyes as she teased him, the light that faded when she realized she had strayed too close to emotion.

The connection they had once shared was not quite so dead as Vivien would like him to believe.

"You know," she said as she began to eat from her own plate. "I heard your brother married."

Benedict hesitated a moment. She was not looking at him but across the expanse of lawn toward the lake. Still, he could feel her awareness of him. She spoke of his family in order to give herself space from whatever brewed between them. He would give it to her, for now.

"Yes, Derek married in the winter and is still awash in newlywed bliss," he responded, still watching her.

She turned toward him, her expression questioning. "Then it was a love match?" she asked, her tone totally incredulous.

Benedict did not understand her disbelief. She had met his brother all of three times during the months they spent together. Two of the times he hadn't even seen them interact beyond an introduction. The third had consisted of mostly polite conversation, though his brother had not hidden his disapproval of the relationship between them.

"I suppose it did not begin that way," he conceded slowly. "Our mother arranged for him to meet his wife, Jocelyn. She comes from a good family of breeding and standing. She is the Duke of Stenbrook's youngest."

Vivien's lips pursed. "Of course she is," she breathed, her voice little more than a whisper.

Benedict shrugged. "And though she certainly fit the description of a perfect match for my brother on paper, I do not think that is what drew them. From the first moment he laid eyes on her a year ago, anyone could see he was smitten. In fact, I would say it took him less than a month to fall deeply in love with the girl."

Vivien's expression did not change and he could read nothing of her reaction to that declaration. "And what of the wife? Is she equally as devoted?"

Benedict nodded. "She seems to be. I do not think he enters a room that she isn't tracking him with her gaze. They seem to be a very happy match indeed."

Vivien was curiously silent for a long moment before she set her half-empty plate aside and wiped her hands on her napkin. "Then I offer them my most sincere felicitations for their union," she said. "Although I assume he must be furious to know you are here with me."

Benedict pursed his lips. "I suppose he might disapprove if he knew."

She laughed but there was an edge to the sound. "Don't you think he will know by tomorrow if he does not already? I would think your brother to be quite resourceful about such things."

Benedict leaned forward. He could see this subject troubled her, a fact he did not understand. "If there is to be trouble tomorrow, Vivien, than I shall handle it tomorrow. I would rather live in this moment while I have it."

He leaned forward to kiss her and in an instant her troubles seemed to fade. She cupped his cheeks and returned the kiss with an abandon that spoke of her need for him.

He dragged her to her feet and motioned for the carriage. As he drew back, he smiled.

"What I would like to do next requires a bit of privacy."

She did not refuse him, but simply followed him to the vehicle and allowed him to help her inside. He gave his driver a brief directive, then joined her and shut and locked the door. She was on his side of the carriage in an instant and the kiss that had begun so sweetly outside immediately spiraled out of control.

She tore at his shirt, desperate in her need to touch him. He doubted he was any better, ratcheting her skirts to her waist, reaching between her legs to touch her where he found her deliciously wet already.

She sighed as he stroked her entrance and the fluttering movements of her hands ceased.

"I have been ready for you since I first saw you in the bookstore," she moaned as he breached her with one finger, two, three.

He blinked as an image filled his mind of throwing her against the bookshelf in the very proper shop and fucking her for all to see. The idea excited him and he drove into her harder, loving the flex of her sheath around his fingers as she gasped. He wanted that same flex about his cock, to make her come while he looked into her face in the increasing darkness of the carriage.

She seemed to read his thoughts, for she fumbled for his trouser buttons, unfastening them with little finesse. He lifted her when she was finished and his hard, ready cock bobbed free of the confines of his breeches. She moaned as he positioned her above him and then lowered herself, inch after wet, hot inch, over him.

She flexed as she took him inside, massaging him wickedly as her body stretched to accommodate his length. He had never been so pleased by a woman's body, not before her nor since their last parting. And he had been punished greatly for that obsession. Even long after she was gone, in his every erotic dream, it was her pussy he took. Now, as he filled her, reality left those dreams far behind.

He flexed his hips to take the last inch of space within her and for a moment they sat perfectly still, staring at each other in the gathering darkness of dusk, panting with pleasure at the joining of their bodies.

He parted his lips to speak, but she didn't allow it. She crushed her mouth to his and began to move over him, effectively silencing any words or even thoughts in his head with the sensations she created.

Even after all this time, Vivien knew what he liked. She moved quickly, rising over him with quick, strong thrusts. Her clitoris ground against his pelvis and he felt her twitch as she gasped at the feeling. He gripped her hips, digging his fingers into her flesh as he guided her harder, faster, out of control.

Finally the muscles in her neck strained and she cried out as release washed over her. Her pussy clenched with it, squeezing him, milking him until he could resist no longer. His seed rushed from him in a powerful explosion of pleasure and he roared with the sensation as he held to her so tight he feared he would steal her breath.

She wrapped her arms around his shoulders and they clung to each other for what seemed like a perfect eternity, but finally she drew away, gave him an awkward smile and moved to the opposite side of the carriage. He watched as she fixed herself, covering what he had revealed and taken pleasure in, smoothing wrinkles and tucking strands of hair away. Within a few moments, she looked as though nothing had happened.

Except for the twinkle of light in her eyes that said they shared a delicious secret.

He half-smiled as he refastened his trousers just as they turned into Vivien's drive and the carriage came to a stop. The door opened and a footman appeared to help her down. She paused once she had reached the ground and the servant stepped away.

She looked at Benedict, her face unreadable as she looked up at him. For a moment, he thought she might ask him to come inside. To continue what had been begun in the carriage. But she shook her head and smiled instead.

"G-Good night," she whispered.

He nodded. She was too hesitant to share more than what had been shared. He knew that about her before and it hadn't changed now.

"Good night," he said softly, but as she turned to enter her home, he called out. "Oh and, Vivien?"

Slowly, she pivoted to face him. "Yes?"

"I'm not selling the carriage. It has too many new memories now." He smiled as he reached out to close the carriage door. The footman climbed up into his place and they pulled away, leaving Vivien gaping at him in her drive.

Benedict laughed as he settled back against the leather seats. At least he knew one thing—he could still stymie Vivien Manning. And that was a feat worth valuing indeed.

CHAPTER 8

Derek arrived early, forcing Benedict from pleasant dreams of Vivien and the day…and night…they had shared. So when he entered the breakfast room, he could not spare his brother a smile, but instead glared at him before he took a plate and began dishing food from the trays on the sideboard.

"I didn't expect you until at least luncheon," he snapped. "I thought you could contain your disapproval until then."

Derek rose from the position he had taken at the head of Benedict's table and folded his arms. "Then you know why I am here."

Benedict pivoted to face his brother. Derek was dressed impeccably, looking as if he had never made a reckless decision in his life. Benedict had never been like him in that regard. He wasn't considered a rake, didn't even aspire to be one, but he too often made choices based on his heart.

As he always had when it came to Vivien.

"I know the purpose of your visit, but I require you to say it out loud," Benedict said. He sat down at the table, set his plate down with a clatter and folded his arms as he stared up at his brother. "Go ahead, you are bursting with your arguments, so make them."

Derek retook his seat and sipped his coffee before he said anything. The delay made Benedict antsy and he shifted in his chair.

"You must have known that news of your meeting with Vivien Manning would get back to me," his brother began softly.

Benedict thought he would have a harsh retort or even a blazing argument when his brother began, but he found, now that her name had been spoken, that the air had been let out of his high emotions.

"I wasn't thinking of you, Brother, I assure you," he said. A statement not entirely true, but true enough.

"You met with her at Mattigan's, I hear. And then the British Museum," his brother continued.

"Spies at both, I assume?" Benedict said as he shoveled a forkful of fluffy eggs into his mouth.

"No, only concerned friends."

Benedict rolled his eyes. "Spies."

"Whatever you call them, I was troubled to hear about it. Benedict, it is one thing to see her at *her* gatherings once every six months and say hello, but to make arrangements to escort her about Town like she is your mistress again…"

"There weren't any arrangements," he said softly. "We met quite by accident and the day developed as it did." He flashed briefly to both their powerful encounters in the carriage and shook away the erotic memories. "Do not make it out to be more than it is."

"And what is it?" Derek asked.

Benedict glanced up from his plate to find his brother's expression soft and filled with concern.

"I don't know," he admitted.

Derek got up and paced the room once. When he returned to the table, he said, "You are a grown man, capable of making your own decisions, of course. I hope you know my worries have nothing to do with my assessment of your sensibleness."

"Of course they do," Benedict laughed, but it was a humorless sound.

"No." Derek shook his head. "They truly do not. I just…I don't want to see you fall back."

Benedict had been keeping his emotions in check, both internally and for the sake of his brother, but suddenly they bubbled forward in a burst he did not expect.

"This is easy for you to judge and to say," he snapped, rising from his own chair. "You are married to your love. You don't know what it feels like to have her torn from you. You cannot judge the reaction you think I should have for the same."

"Benedict—" his brother began in that pitying tone that Benedict hated more than any other.

"No," he snapped out in interruption. "I realize you have your opinions. I respect them, for I know they come from the best of intentions. But I am not a fool. I am doing this with Vivien because once it is over, it's over."

His brother blinked and he saw a dawning of understanding on Derek's face. And more of that cursed pity, as well.

"I do not want to see you filled with regret," his brother said softly.

Benedict frowned. He might deny it to his sibling, but in truth that was his private fear as well. Already he was beginning to feel those same deeper emotions for Vivien that he had once before. Losing her a second time was bound to hurt.

"No," he said, almost more for himself than for Derek. "I refuse to regret anything. This time I *know* this affair is over, even before it began. My only regret would be if I didn't say yes."

Derek moved toward him, but Benedict held up a hand to stop him.

"Please," he said. "Stop being my older brother. Stop trying to protect me. Just…leave it be."

Derek's face revealed how difficult a request that was for him. In some ways, Benedict appreciated that. Appreciated that his brother longed to help him. To keep him from harm as he had when they were mere children.

But in this, especially this, Benedict had to make his own decisions. And suffer their consequences, no matter what they were.

~

Vivien sipped her tea and tried to maintain some kind of decorum as she looked across the table at Mariah and Lysandra. It was a difficult task when her mind returned again and again to thoughts of Benedict. And not just the way he had touched her, filled her, but of their talk all the previous day.

Despite her attempts to maintain distance, she felt closer to him, probably more than she ever had, even when they were lovers in the past.

"And away she goes again," Lysandra laughed. "Vivien, are you certain you wish to have this meeting? You are obviously distracted."

Vivien dragged herself to the present. She was never *obviously* anything! That was a skill she had forced herself to perfect in order to protect herself from those around her. If her emotions were clear, she was failing indeed.

"Of course we must have the meeting," she said, far more sharply than she had intended. "The Charitable Fund for Young Ladies is too important not to give it my full attention."

Lysandra's laughter faded. "It is a good cause. And I thank you both for allowing me to be involved. As you know, I lost everything and if it were not for you, Vivien, my life might have become quite desperate."

The sharpness Vivien had forced faded slightly. She had begun the Charitable Fund for Young Ladies just after Lysandra's marriage and put her in charge of it. The money was Vivien's, but the respectability came from the ladies of Society who ran the galas and raised the awareness of the women who were forced onto the street by circumstance. If she could save just one from a life of desperation...from a life like her own had once been...she felt like she had done something important.

And that was even more significant now that she intended to leave London.

"I do wish you could be a public part of the organization," Lysandra sighed.

Vivien shook her head. "If I were even suspected as being its benefactress, the entire endeavor would collapse. The other Society ladies wouldn't want to sully their hands and reputations by associating with me and my dirty money."

Mariah sighed. Although Lysandra had only briefly been a mistress, and only to the man she ultimately married, Mariah had been closer to Vivien's own position. Her transition into Society after her marriage to John Rycroft was proving more difficult, though her friend never complained.

Vivien could see hers would be impossible, even if she wished to attempt it.

"I fear Vivien is right," Mariah gently explained to Lysandra. "From my own experiences, I know it takes a great deal of work to make any friends at all once you've been in our position. I'm lucky that a handful of ladies, including your sister-in-law, Lysandra, have welcomed me and made things easier."

"Those in the *ton* value their respectability too highly to risk calling a whore a friend," Vivien mused. "I accept that, so there is no use belaboring the point."

Lysandra opened her mouth to argue further, but Vivien did not allow it. "At any rate, your plans for the gala to raise more funds for the transitional home for these women sound perfect. You must tell me all about the night once it happens."

She got to her feet and paced away so her friends wouldn't see how troubling this subject was to her. In truth, she wished she could make herself as blind to that fact. She knew what she was, she recognized the consequences, but it seemed that being with Benedict made them all the harder.

She turned with a false smile. "Is that all?"

"I have one more point that has to do with…well, not the charity exactly, but the purpose behind it," Mariah said.

Vivien tensed. She could see her friend's anxiety and it made her just as anxious in return. "Go ahead."

"I have it on good authority that the Earl of Dersingham is back to his old tricks."

Vivien squeezed her eyes shut as Lysandra made a pained sound in her throat.

"You mean, I suppose, that he is abusing the servants again, knowing they cannot escape without his reference?" Lysandra asked softly.

Mariah's lips thinned as she nodded. "Yes."

Lysandra pushed back from the table and walked away across the room. Mariah and Vivien exchanged a glance of concern, though neither of them said a thing. These kinds of stories hit their friend harder, for she had been in a similar position once. It was why the charity they had formed was so important to her.

"And was the girl…raped…as the last two were?" Lysandra whispered.

Mariah nodded again. "She told a friend, another servant in another house, and the story came to me through the usual servant channels."

"Is there any way to get the girl out?" Vivien asked.

Mariah shook her head. "I have used up all my resources for housemaids. Until we get the school off the ground, we cannot even remove them from the situation."

Vivien squeezed her hands into fists in her lap. One of the items on her list of things to do was to destroy someone evil. And there seemed to be no one who deserved being destroyed more than the Earl of Dersingham. Publicly and thoroughly.

"I will call in a favor about the girl," Vivien said, her voice cracking.

"And what about the next girl?" Lysandra whispered.

Vivien got to her feet and moved to wrap an arm around her friend. "I will find a way to take care of her too."

Lysandra squeezed her waist gently. "I'm certain we will try," she said and pulled away, pain in her stare.

Vivien ground her teeth. She was definitely going to destroy the man. For Lysandra and any other woman like her who had ever turned to desperation to escape from horror. She owed them all that and more.

Lysandra turned to look at them and a smile now covered her pain. "Now that the business talk is over, there must be something personal to discuss. I do not wish to leave here on such a painful note."

Mariah laughed, though she, too, looked strained by the previous topic. "Oh good, I was wondering when we would reach the point of gossip. And I think someone in this very room has some to share."

Vivien looked at Lysandra. "You do?"

Lysandra shook her head and shot a glance at Mariah in question. "What about me?"

Mariah barked out a laugh. "Oh no. Not our dear Lysandra. You, *Vivien*."

Lysandra's troubled expression cleared. "Vivien always has the best gossip. What is the latest, then?"

Vivien shrugged. "I have no idea what Mariah is talking about, I assure you."

"I do not speak of common gossip," Mariah said with a glare. "I am referring to you and Benedict Greystone."

Lysandra pivoted to stare at Vivien in shock. "Your former lover, Benedict Greystone?"

Mariah shook her head. "Not a mere lover, my dear. Greystone was the very last protector Vivien ever had. It is rumored they have perhaps renewed their relationship."

Vivien flinched as Lysandra's mouth dropped open. "I had no

idea he was your *final* protector! But you are with him again... I thought you had no wish to ever have a protector again."

"I don't," Vivien managed through clenched teeth. "He isn't my protector."

Lysandra blinked. "But he is your lover again?"

Vivien wished she could deny it, but what would be the use? "Yes. But there is little else to say on the subject. I have taken lovers before without this kind of badgering."

Mariah lifted her eyebrows. "Yes, you have, but never with someone like Greystone. You truly have no intention of addressing the issue of your renewed affair with him or any other feelings you have on the matter of him?"

"No," Vivien snapped, more emotionally than perhaps she had desired. "I do not wish to discuss it."

Mariah pressed her lips together and stared at her friend in surprise. "I see," she said after a moment.

Vivien held back a curse. Now she was showing too much emotion again, something that had never been a problem up until Benedict came crashing back into her life.

"Honestly," she said, softening her tone significantly. "There is nothing to discuss. Just as I attempt to do with all my lovers, Benedict and I have always remained friends. If we have shared anything more recently than an exchange of hellos, please do not read too much into it. We already know where a relationship will end. I don't think either of us is interested in something more."

She said the words she thought she meant, but they tasted very bitter as they passed her lips. True, but bitter.

She smoothed her skirt reflexively and said, "At any rate, I'm so glad we could meet today."

The not-so-subtle hint worked, for Lysandra moved toward the door with a troubled gaze. In the foyer, she embraced Vivien. Vivien could see there was something she wanted to say, but instead she said her farewells to Mariah and headed for her carriage.

Mariah embraced her and the hug was tight. Before they parted she whispered, "Someday I hope you'll let *someone* in, Vivien. Me…her…him…just someone. I have learned that it is worth the risk."

Vivien drew back with a shrug. "My dear, you are in as far as anyone could get, I assure you. I will speak to you soon."

Mariah nodded and left her standing alone in her foyer. But as she closed the door on the sight of her friends' carriages departing the drive, an emptiness consumed her that no one could fill.

Because even if Mariah wished it, Vivien could never allow anyone in fully. It wasn't possible.

CHAPTER 9

Benedict paced Vivien's parlor, barely seeing her naughty red wallpaper with its imbedded images of couples engaging in sex acts. His mind was too busy to attend to such things.

He had put off seeing her. In truth, that had been a test to see how long he could do it. It seemed two days was his limit now before the ache to touch her, taste her, feel her body and hear her voice was unbearable.

He cursed as he glanced at the clock. He had been waiting all of five minutes and it felt like an eternity. His brother was right—he was in too deep, drowning in his feelings for her. No good could come of it.

But he was still here. Where he wanted to be more than anything in the world, even if it was to his detriment to surrender to her siren's call.

The door to the chamber opened and he spun around to watch Vivien enter the room. She was wearing a pretty red gown, cut daringly low so that he got a very nice look at the soft roundness of her cleavage. Her blonde hair was done up loosely and thick waves of it moved around her face, framing the angles of her cheekbones and the brightness of her blue eyes.

"Benedict," she breathed as she closed the door behind her.

Her tone was so welcoming, so warm, so desperate…as if she had been missing him as much as he missed her. Not that he would ever expect her to admit such a thing. Vivien saw love as weakness.

But passion *was* something she would accept and return, so he poured it into her as he crossed the room in a handful of long steps and dragged her against him for a kiss that melted his very bones.

She moaned against his mouth and clung to him with both her arms, pulling him against her, writhing as they kissed for what seemed like an eternity.

But he wanted more. He wanted all of her, everything in her heart, her soul, her body. But she would give only one of those three, so he dove into the taking with fervor. He stepped back and swiftly went to work on the gown she wore. There were only three buttons on the front, just enough to hold in the bounty of her bosom but little else. He stripped them open with a flick of his wrist and revealed that she wore no undergarments beneath.

A fact that made his cock all the harder as he stared at the smooth curves of her breast, the hint of her nipple as the silky fabric slid away from the swells.

"No shift?" he murmured.

She shrugged. "I hoped you would come to me tonight."

"Are you admitting you missed me?" he asked, teasing but needing to hear an affirmation that this madness between them was not his alone.

She didn't answer, but slid her arms from the gown and shimmied it slowly down her body, revealing herself inch by inch until she stood before him in only her stockings and slippers.

"Shall I take that as a yes?" he grunted past a dry throat.

She smiled wickedly. "By all means, *take* it."

He moved on her, but this time he didn't crush her body to his. He pushed her back until she fell against the length of a fainting couch specifically built for the very pleasures he readied himself to indulge in. A fainting couch he had taken her on a dozen times in what seemed like another life.

Tonight he reclaimed that life. Even for just a moment.

He dropped down on his knees before her and grasped her hips to drag her to the end of the couch. She stared down the length of her body at him, blue eyes dark and sparkling with desire and passion. With *need*.

A need he intended to slake thoroughly.

"I have longed to taste you," he whispered as he pulled the slipper off one foot, then the other and slowly rolled her stockings off her legs, kissing her knee, her ankle as he did so. "To enjoy the flavor that fills my mouth in my dreams."

She sucked in a breath of surprise and her eyes went wide above him.

"That surprises you," he continued, opening her legs wide to reveal the slick and glistening sex that awaited him. "That I continue to dream about you, your body, about taking you in every way imaginable."

She hesitated, but finally nodded wordlessly.

"It shouldn't. I would wager any man who has touched you would be branded by the action. Would be changed irreparably."

He stopped talking as he reached out to stroke a finger along her entrance. She was so hot and wet that his cock actually twitched within the confines of his trousers.

He leaned over her, spreading her open with his thumbs before he pressed his mouth to her sex. She gasped and arched toward him, a tiny loss of control that he reveled in as he began the work to bring her to orgasm with fervor. He stroked his tongue over her, sucking at her clitoris, driving into her body with little shallow strokes.

Vivien cried out with the increasing pressure and rhythm of his ministrations, grabbing at the smooth fabric of the settee, lifting her body to meet him in helpless abandon until finally she gasped out, "Please!"

It was just one word, a very ordinary word, but Benedict lifted his gaze in shock as she said it. Vivien, begging? That had certainly never happened before, not any of the many times they fell into bed together. Normally she had more restraint than that.

But now she stared at him, eyes wide and pleading, and he realized something was different now. Something had shifted between them.

He was breaking down her walls.

He smiled and lowered his mouth to her. Gently, he sucked her clitoris, rolling his tongue around and around the little nub as she gasped and moaned above him with sounds of near release. He built his tempo and when he slid one thick finger inside her as he continued to suck, she screamed out his name in the quiet parlor and her body jolted with an orgasm that shuddered through her entire body.

As her crisis faded, she flopped back against the settee cushions and looked up at him through a hooded gaze. For a long time, they were both silent and then she sat up partially and smiled at him.

"How long are you going to remain clothed?" she whispered, her tone wicked and teasing.

He grinned and got up to strip down with record speed. When he was naked before her, she slid to the edge of the couch and took him in hand, stroking over him once, twice, three times.

He dipped his head over his shoulders and groaned as lightning bursts of pleasure jolted up his cock from her touch. She had a certain expression and he knew that her intention was to take him into her mouth, just as he had done. It would feel amazing, but he wanted something more intimate with her. He wanted to look into her eyes as he drove into her body, felt her flex around him in welcome and surrender.

He pulled away and dropped down to pin her against the settee. She looked up at him, slightly pouting, even though her blue eyes were bright with anticipation of what he would do.

"You don't want my mouth?" she purred.

He kissed her, let her taste her own earthy flavors on his lips and tongue. She moaned against him and her legs parted wider. He nudged his cock at her entrance, its wet heat taunting him with what he would have in just a few short moments.

"I want everything," he moaned and slid into her sheath in one long, languid thrust.

She shut her eyes and lifted toward him, her sex gripping him as if she couldn't get enough. He pressed his lips to hers a second time and began to kiss her, stroking her tongue with his as he stroked her body with his. She relaxed in his arms, lifting to greet him, arching her hips to his and clinging to his shoulders as if she would wash away if not grounded.

He drove a little faster, taking and claiming while the pleasure of her body rushed through him, overwhelmed him. He felt release building deep within his loins and he struggled to control himself as he felt her drive toward orgasm. Suddenly her eyes flew open and she tensed against his chest, smashing her breasts to him as she opened her mouth and cried out. Her hips flexed wildly and her release was evident by her face, her body, her nails digging into his shoulders.

Seeing her come was just too much and he lost control. Pleasure exploded within him, blurring his vision as his hips slammed without finesse or rhythm against hers and his hot seed filled her. He collapsed against her, breath coming in pants, and he held her to him for a long moment.

Finally, his world stopped tilting and he realized he still crushed her to the settee. With a grunt, he parted their bodies and flopped onto his back. She curled against his side and they remained silent together in the quiet.

Benedict stared up at the ceiling high above. Even the moldings were done in erotic images of bodies intertwined. He shook his head with a smile as he shifted his focus back to the naked woman in his arms.

Although they had certainly shared long nights when they were last lovers, Vivien had never been comfortable being held. She found means of escape and built walls whenever he offered her tenderness rather than passion.

Tonight, she rested her head in the crook of his shoulder, gently tracing patterns across his skin, and made no effort to remove herself from the intimacy of their embrace.

"May I ask you something?" she finally said when they had been silent for several moments.

He braced himself for the ramifications of all the questions she could have, but nodded. "Of course. You may ask me anything."

She looked up at him at his words and there was a flash of sudden, deep emotion in her eyes that she immediately masked. "What do you know of the Earl of Dershingham?"

Benedict hesitated. That was *not* one of the questions for which he had prepared a moment ago. He hardly knew how to answer it except honestly, for he did not understand her reasons behind it.

"We do not move in the same circles, so I have little cause to interact with the man, but I have never heard anything good," he said softly.

She stared into the fire across the room. "Nor have I."

There was a wistfulness to her tone, but also an anger. Neither of which he understood.

"Please tell me you are not asking for my help in shopping for a new protector," he said, his tone light even though he was utterly serious in his words. "Especially not after the passion we just shared."

She stared at him in horror. "Dear God, no!"

She sat up, offering him the most magnificent view of her naked breasts, the curve of her bare arms, the sweetness of her tousled hair down around her face.

He smiled. The strength of her resolve told him everything he needed to know about the truth of her statement. "Then why do you ask me about this man?"

She drew her lip between her teeth and worried it as she stared at him, unflinching. For once, he could see the full course of her thoughts. She considered the truth, but hesitated. She wanted to pull away and distance herself from honesty and connection.

He reached out to take her hand and smoothed his fingers over her palms gently. "Please," he whispered.

Vivien had never weakened to him. There were a few times he thought she might over the years, but something in her had always stopped her. Tonight, in the sparkling light of the fire, with his hand in hers, she couldn't seem to harden her heart or protect her privacy or whatever it was that drove her to build so many walls between herself and anyone else who might see inside.

She tilted her head, looked him straight in the eye and said, "I wish to destroy him."

~

Vivien shook her head as the words left her lips. What had she just done? Shared something from her private list of things to do? With *him*?

She shook his hand away and managed to push past him to her feet. She pulled her gown over her naked, flushed body and fastened the little buttons along the front without looking at him. Still, she felt his shocked stare burn into her back. And not just shocked at what she'd said, but that she had shared something so unexpected and personal.

It was not her way, and for good reason.

"Are you going to say something?" she asked, hardening herself as she spun on him.

He stared up at her, but his expression was unreadable. Funny how they could reverse roles like that, her with her emotions wild, him calm and inscrutable.

"No one deserves to be destroyed more than Dershingham," he conceded.

Her eyes went wide. That was all?

But of course, it was not. Benedict sat up, still entirely naked and utterly distracting.

"But what you suggest is madness, Vivien. A woman of your position—"

She cut him off with a wave of her hand. "A woman of my position is the *only* kind who could stand up to someone like him."

He continued to stare at her with such focus that she felt the uncommon sensation of blood rushing to her cheeks. She turned away so he would not see it.

"I only meant that there would be a cost if you did so," he said softly.

"Yes," she agreed, thinking of all the consequences that would very likely follow a public destruction of an important man. Funny how they did not trouble her anymore. The pain that would follow the action would be very brief since she intended to leave London.

Benedict got up and continued, unaware of her thoughts. "You have built a life, a reputation, on your discretion. If you swing on this man, especially in a way that will be seen as public, you could violently alter your future."

Vivien mulled those words. Violently alter her future. Yes, that sounded perfect.

She turned on him.

"You say no one deserves destruction more—does that mean you know what he does?" she asked.

Benedict shrugged. "He's a cheat at cards, a miser with his family, there was some talk about a duel where the man opposite him was shot and permanently maimed under very questionable circumstances..."

When she shook her head, he trailed off.

"These are minor transgressions," she whispered. "It is the servants who receive the worst consequences of his evil. Girls in his employ, especially the youngest of them..." She cleared her throat and blinked at a sudden sting behind her eyes. "Raped. Brutalized and tortured. If they try to leave, they are given poor references and cannot find new employment."

Benedict stepped back in shock, but his expression didn't slow her pace. She continued, her voice cracking with emotion she could not control as the awful words continued to spill forth.

"Some have had no choice but the streets as their escape. Others have remained in his employ. One girl killed herself last year, swallowed poison from the house and lived her last few days in agony in a *barn* because the bastard didn't want to hear her cries in his halls, disturbing his supper. She was but fifteen at her death."

Benedict sucked in a breath and reached for his trousers. Once he was clothed, he shook his head. "I am shocked at this. Everyone knows he is a bastard, but these allegations are much darker than any leveled at him before."

"But why would men of your rank know?" she asked with a shake of her head. "It isn't as if servants take up much space in your mind, do they? Once they disappear below stairs, you forget them entirely. And that is the notion these predators rely upon. No one cares, so no one will stop their behavior. But those of us who walk outside your world, who are closer to servant than to lady of the manor, we know the truth. And I am tired of remaining silent."

He stared at her for a long moment, his expression unreadable, but then his eyes widened and his thoughts became clear. He might hesitate to support her wild plan to destroy a man of rank...but he *admired* her for the desire to do so. Admired her! She did not think anyone had done that for years, at least not a man.

His regard warmed her unexpectedly and she turned her face so that he wouldn't see how meaningful his support was to her. There was no use giving him so much power.

"What if I...helped you?" he asked when he next spoke.

That question forced her to pivot in shock to stare at him. "Help me?" she repeated, the words seeming foreign on her tongue.

He laughed. "Yes, *help* you. Surely you have heard the term before. It means to come to your aid, be a partner in your plans, render assistance—"

She lifted a hand to still his teasing words. "Yes, I know what the word *help* means, Benedict! But you cannot be serious."

"I am utterly serious," he said, his brow wrinkling with trouble and confusion.

"It is a noble suggestion, of course, but it could only bring you grief. Do not forget, you have a reputation that is even more steeped in your actions than mine is. Your family, your *brother*, they will surely disapprove, as will three-quarters of the *ton*, even if they discovered the truth of what the bastard is doing."

Benedict pursed his lips. "You think so little of those of my rank."

"I have known a great many of them," she said, her tone filled with more bitterness than perhaps she had intended.

He frowned. "So you lump me in with them, then?"

Her lips parted at the true hurt in his expression. And her surprise extended to her own reaction, as well. In truth, she did not put Benedict in the same category as his cohorts. She never had.

"No," she said, reaching for his hand despite the danger in touching him during this highly charged exchange. "Of course not."

"Then will you not allow that perhaps *I* am tired of remaining silent, as well? Injustice should not be tolerated by anyone!"

She pursed her lips as she tried to think of some way to dissuade him from joining her cause. For both their sakes. But she could think of none save one.

"And you are looking for a wife," she said, trying to maintain some tone of innocence as she brought up the subject. "Women like a hero."

She hoped that her reminder would set him back from this course she intended to follow. And when his face fell slightly, she thought her reminder had done just that.

He moved toward her and lifted her hand to his chest. "Let us not speak about wives."

She blinked. Some part of her recognized that she should do just what he asked her not to do. She should press on the subject of his intention to marry until it drove him away.

But she couldn't. Even if she should, even if he needed to hear it, even if there were a thousand reasons. She couldn't. There was something in Benedict, just as there had always been, that made her surrender.

"Then shall we talk about our takedown of the bastard instead?" she whispered, suddenly aware of how close they were, how he was still shirtless, how her body reacted to his heat and his scent.

He shook his head, leaning closer. "Later," he murmured.

Then his mouth was on hers again and she spiraled into a dark cavern of pleasure where nothing else existed but them.

CHAPTER 10

Benedict set one book back on Vivien's shelf and reached for another. His eyes went wide at what was within. The shelves in her public parlors were lined with erotic tomes, complete with illustrations of a most shocking nature. That, combined with her erotic art and wallpaper, made his head spin.

But he had always known that his lover was a sensual woman, unafraid of intimacy of the body. No, what she was afraid of was something far deeper— intimacy of the mind and the spirit. Sharing anything, even the smallest detail, of the woman behind her public persona, was terrifying to her. So she built walls with her clothing, her sensuality, her shocking chambers where sin was king…

He knew she had private rooms in this house…she had to, no one could sleep full-time in that gargantuan bed she shared with her lovers. *Those* were the chambers he wanted to see, a glimpse of her real self, her real life when she was alone and not trying to impress those with power.

She would never show him of her own volition, but he had a plan to get around her barriers this time.

The door behind him opened and he turned to watch her come into the room. Her blonde hair was swept up in a complicated fashion and her bright blue eyes were accentuated by the equally stunning blue of her gown.

"Good afternoon," he said with a slight bow in her direction.

She laughed. "We are very proper today."

"I always greet a lady properly," he said, then crossed the room and took her arm to pull her close. After he kissed her slowly, thoroughly, he smiled. "You see?"

She staggered slightly as he released her and smoothed her dress gently. "Ah, yes. Though I doubt you were taught the second welcome in a comportment session."

"You never met my governess," he said, then whistled.

Her eyes went wide. "You cannot be serious!"

He shook his head. "I admit, I am not. But for a moment you thought me as wicked as some of the men who come to your home regularly."

She smiled, but the expression seemed forced. "Some of those men are very nice, yes, but I would not want them to stay longer than an evening, I assure you. Their wickedness is not their most charming trait. Though everyone seems to think that is all I care about."

He tilted his head. She seemed truly irritated by what had been honest teasing. Which created an opportunity for him to press for those details he was always so hungry for.

"If wickedness is not the dominant trait you look for in a gentleman, then what is?"

She hesitated for so long that he wondered if she had actually heard his question, but then she sighed. Her gaze was far away as she murmured, "I could scarcely tell you anymore."

He frowned. "Your tone speaks of regret."

She darted her gaze to him, wild and unsteady. "Of course not, don't be foolish. I do not live my life with regret—it is a waste of time."

"Sadness, then, if you prefer the word." He shrugged. "Deny it all you like, but I see it in your eyes. I would offer you comfort if you would take it."

She stiffened and moved away. "No. I'm fine. Of course, I'm fine. I doubt you came to call on me with the purpose of analyzing my thoughts on men or regret."

He paused. Actually, both those topics sounded like perfectly reasonable ones for them to dissect. At least they were personal. But he wouldn't say so if he wished to stay.

"I have come because I've been thinking of our conversation from two days past about the Earl of Dersingham."

Her chin jerked up at that and interest pushed away the warning in her eyes. "Have you?"

He nodded. "I believe I've come up with a way to destroy him, if that is still your desire."

Her spine straightened and she moved toward him a few steps. "It is! What is your plan?"

He drew in a breath. "Well, my dear, I'm afraid my answer isn't going to be as simple as all that."

Her brow wrinkled. "What does that mean, Benedict?"

"If I'm going to help you, I'm afraid I must ask for something in return." He folded his arms and looked at her evenly.

Her face, which had been lit up with excitement, slowly fell, went flat, emotionless. "It's obvious you may have your way with me whenever you like— there is no need to bribe. Is there some deviant act you wish to perform or wish me to perform? Tell me, but don't play foolish games beneath you."

Inside, his heart hurt. That she had been bribed like this, for her body before, made him ache. That she lumped him in with those who had done so made him sick.

"What I want has nothing to do with your body," he said, shrugging so his real thoughts wouldn't be too clear. "I would hope you know me better than that. If I want you, I will tell you and respect what your answer is, whether it's yes or no. I think I proved that by walking away all those years ago, didn't I?"

Her lips parted and whatever skill she had at pretending her emotions away failed. He could see her shock that he would put things so plainly and her pain at the memory of their parting. So she had been hurt, too. Somehow that was a small comfort to him.

"I'm sorry," she whispered. "I should not have jumped to a foolish conclusion when I do know you better. You have never proven yourself to be so cold."

"Thank you."

She shifted with discomfort. "If it is not sensual, then what is it you wish to trade for your plan?"

He drew a deep breath. "I want to see your chambers."

After a moment filled with only her confused expression, she shook her head. "I don't know what you mean. You've been to my chamber dozens of times, more than dozens. How would that be a boon for you?"

"Your *real* chambers, Vivien. The ones that have nothing to do with your role as mistress, as courtesan, as celebrated matchmaker to protectors everywhere."

She swallowed hard and backed away a step. "And what makes you think I have chambers such as those you describe?"

He laughed. "Come, my dear, you just admitted you know me, and you must admit I know you too. Not as well as I would like, but more than your average lover has. That fact is part of why you sent me away all those years ago."

She drew in a breath to speak, but he held up a hand to stop her.

"There is no use arguing the point when we both know it is true," he said. "I only mean that I can see where you exist and where you don't. You don't exist in these chambers, in the bedroom where you take your lovers."

"Of course I do," she protested, throwing up her hands and walking away. It was a dramatic gesture, but one meant to keep him from seeing her face.

"No, you do not," he insisted, maneuvering so that she had to look at him again. "I know you like books, that you like the kind of art you see in the British Museum. None of those pursuits are found here. These chambers only contain images and hints that are part of a mask you wear."

Her gaze slipped to the floor and for a long time she was quiet. "Perhaps you are wrong about me. There may be nothing more to me than the mask you claim I wear and these chambers are an exact reflection of my true self."

He had taken her aback with his accusations and he could see she was less equipped to battle him at present. Which was why this was the perfect time to strike, to invade her privacy.

"I *know* that isn't true," he said, his voice hardly more than a whisper. He cupped her chin and tilted her face up to hold her stare. She shifted with discomfort beneath its scrutiny. "That is my request, Vivien. You show me a glimpse of what you hide from all others, and I will tell you my plan to destroy Dersingham."

For a moment, he thought she would refuse. That her desire to hold herself away from anyone who might get close was stronger than her desire for some kind of justice against the Evil Earl, as he had begun to call Dersingham in his head. But then her shoulders slumped.

"Very well," she sighed. "If seeing a handful of boring rooms is all the payment you require, then come with me and I will oblige your odd request."

She pivoted on her heel and walked from the room at a swift clip he had to hurry to keep up with. She did not look back to mark his progress but simply moved up the stairs toward the bedroom he, and others before and since him, had seen for years. He pursed his lips as she hesitated in her movement at the door. She wasn't about to pass off this place as her real chamber, was she?

Instead, she turned to him. "What you have sought has always been closer than you imagined," she said, lifting her chin as if this confession would be used against her. "The chamber here that you have seen is connected to my real bedchamber, through the door in the dressing room. It locks automatically behind me so that my lovers have no access without the key, which is hidden. I will not tell you where."

Benedict lifted his eyebrows in surprise. "Why have your chambers so close?"

She laughed, though the sound was hollow. "Do you think I wish to stream half-naked through the whole house to return to my bed after I spend the night with a man? I do try not to shock the servants too regularly. It isn't fair to them."

Benedict nodded and followed her a short way down the hall to the next door. There she produced a key from a hidden pocket in her gown and opened the door. As she stepped back to motion him in, he took a breath.

The chamber she made public was dominated by a bed and nothing more. It was created for sin and sin was all that occurred there. But this room was something far different. It was a true place where a woman would sleep, dress, live, dream. And it was so very Vivien to its core.

The walls were done in a soft, pretty green paint and covered with white wainscoting. The bed was comfortable by its looks, but not the massive feat of sensual bliss that was just two rooms away. Still, it would fit two quite nicely.

A dressing table was set across from the bed, with a bottle of rosewater and a hairbrush and a few other items that were private to Vivien. He moved toward the bed to see the book on her end table. As he picked it up, a piece of paper beneath it fluttered to the ground.

He stooped to pick it up, but Vivien rushed over and snatched it away before he could touch it or read anything more than the term "Loose Ends" in its title. He stared as she snatched the sheet against her chest.

"That is private," she snapped.

He wrinkled his brow. "Loose ends?"

Her face paled and she shook her head. "Just a few items I need to take care of before I—before the Season ends."

He shifted at her sudden attitude. Perhaps it was because they were in her real chamber and that fact made her vulnerable and uncomfortable, but there was fear in her stare now. Anxiety he couldn't place the cause of.

She turned away and shoved the paper in a drawer of her dressing table, then pivoted back to face him. "Now I have done as you asked. You have seen my chambers, though I do not understand your purpose for wishing to do so. I would like to hear the plan you have formulated for our dear friend Dersingham."

He stepped back in order to give her space in her obvious discomfort. She seemed to appreciate the gesture, for some of the high color left her cheeks.

"Our dear friend Dersingham," he chuckled as he took a place on a settee before her fire.

She shifted as he made himself comfortable in her chamber, but did not protest. He took that as the most encouragement he was likely to receive and plowed on.

"Did you know he is almost bankrupt?"

Her eyebrows lifted. "No!"

He nodded.

"But how have I not heard this?" she asked, pacing toward him with fingers clenched at her sides. "I do not wish to sound like a braggart, but the fact is that when a man is destitute, I do hear of that fact. My network of spies is enormous!"

Benedict shrugged one shoulder. "I imagine that is true, but you see, Dersingham has hidden the facts very well. He lies to one creditor to pay another, he continues to live at the same level as he always has. Even his wife does not know of their dire situation."

She pursed her lips. "I would think his wife does not know very much at all if she would put up with the depravity of his actions. At least, I would hope she did not."

Benedict nodded, though in his heart he had to think that Lady Dersingham might not know about the money, but she surely knew about the servants. Whether she cared about their plight or contributed to it was another story.

"But if the facts of his despair are not well-known, how have you come across them?" she asked.

He smiled. "You are not the only one with a network of spies."

She tilted her head in disbelief. "And why would you need spies?"

"A gentleman of my position must know as much as a lady of yours," he admitted. "For investment purposes, so I wouldn't be taken advantage of, that sort of thing. I have a financial interest that is shared by Dersingham and when I spoke to a third party involved, they shared a piece of information. Once I started to follow that lead, more and more people began to share their own tiny bits of knowledge. The complete picture is…" He drew a long breath. "Very harsh. Dersingham would be ruined if the truth came out about his debts."

"Good," Vivien said softly.

There was no mistaking the dark pleasure she felt in Dersingham's misfortunes. A dark pleasure that went beyond justice for a few servants she had never met. It made him wonder, once again, what she had endured herself that made her want to hurt the Earl so much.

"But how could his financial misfortunes benefit us?" she asked with a tilt of her head.

"Dersingham has a son about my age, you know. He has arranged a union for him that could sturdy the family coffers. The young lady in question is an American named Felicity Beecher."

Vivien could not contain her surprise. "Why, even I've heard of her! Her father has more money than God and has been bent on matching her with a title since he first visited London last year."

Benedict nodded. "Beecher does value the title—he's quite uncouth about his drives in that arena. *But* he is also a bit of a prig when it comes to propriety and his little angel of a daughter. I believe if he had a whiff of any kind of scandal surrounding Dersingham, such as his financial woes, his sexual conquests or even perhaps a rumor about the son…"

Vivien's grin widened. "It would ruin everything!"

"If the marriage falls through, then within the year, Dersingham would not be able to afford a servant, let alone abuse one," Benedict said with a nod.

Vivien clasped her hands together, her eyes lit up like diamonds as she let that statement sink in. He could only stare at how beautiful she looked, how happy he had made her with this information. How he wished it did not take plots of revenge to do so.

"What do you think?" he dared to ask, though he knew the question would break some of the magic of this moment.

She nodded. "I think it is brilliant. But I do worry about the women currently in his employ. He could become worse in his abuse if the noose is tightening around his neck. The kind of attacks he commits are more about power than pleasure and I could only assist a few at most if that happens. I've used up the bulk of my connections."

Benedict blinked at her concern. He hadn't really thought about the servants she had planned to help with this arrangement and she was correct to worry for them. But that was one place where he knew he could assist.

"I have connections of my own, you know," he said. "My own household could hire some. My family is always on the lookout for good housemaids and there are friends who roam in far different circles than the ones we have shared. As soon as the damage is done to Dersingham, I could arrange to have the staff wooed away at once." He shrugged. "An exodus of servants timed properly with a public humiliation can only make his situation all the worse."

Vivien nodded. "Indeed, and those who have suffered at his hand would have to appreciate that little irony."

He got to his feet and moved toward her for the first time since he had begun to recite his plan. He saw her tense with caution, but there was also invitation and pleasure in her stare. She wanted him, despite her need to keep him at arm's length.

"You know, if you like you could be the one to nail his coffin," he said, tone seductive.

She hesitated before she responded. "How?"

"I am invited to a fete where Mr. Beecher and Miss Felicity will be in attendance. In fact, I have heard they intend to announce the betrothal at this very party. If you accompanied me, *you* could plant the seed with Beecher that will destroy all of Dersingham's hopes."

He expected the joy that had been on her face to double at this last suggestion, but instead her smile fell and she backed away with a hurried step.

"Go with you to a Society party?" She paled three shades. "No, no, it would be highly improper."

He looked at her in true wonder. Vivien was a host of contradictions, at once so certain and yet so tentative.

"But oh-so entertaining," he responded, his voice calm in order to soothe her.

"I wouldn't belong there," she insisted.

"Men take their mistresses to Society gatherings from time to time, surely you have been taken to them before. But if you are suddenly frightened—"

She caught her breath. "I am not afraid of anything!" she snapped, rising to his bait perfectly.

He arched a brow. "You are afraid of any feeling deeper than desire."

He hadn't meant to say such a volatile thing, to tweak her about that subject, especially not when they had just reached a new level of comfort between them.

Just as he expected, Vivien turned her face with a sigh. "Benedict —" she began, her voice soft and tired.

He shook his head and reached for her to keep her from walking away from him.

"But it doesn't matter, does it?" he pressed gently. "We are sharing passion, not anything more. So I ask you for your body if you won't give anything deeper."

Her gaze lifted with a wickedness that jolted to his very core, hardened his cock and made him achy with desire.

"That is one thing you don't have to ask for," she teased, moving closer so that her breath brushed his lips. "We can retire to the other bedchamber right now and—"

"No, I'm afraid that will not do," he interrupted. "Here. I want to make love to you *here*."

CHAPTER 11

Vivien was reeling, though she felt she was doing a reasonable job of keeping that fact to herself. From Benedict's demands to see this very private place, to her strange desire to give him what he asked for, to his detailed plan on how to destroy an Earl, to his declaration that she feared emotion…

None of it made her feel safe or settled. All of it left her confused and trapped in the corner by his boldness.

"Make love here?" she asked, and her voice shook against her will.

He did not respond with words, but merely nodded his head slowly.

She freed her arm from his gentle hold and backed away. "But this is *my* chamber."

He smiled. "We've made love in your chambers before."

She pursed her lips, for he was purposefully mistaking her meaning. Forcing her to say out loud words that were best kept unspoken.

"Not in this chamber," she said, lifting her gaze to meet his with the dignity she kept no matter what her station or situation. Sometimes that dignity had been all she had.

"And why not?" he asked, equally quiet.

She shook her head, partly in frustration and partly in continued refusal.

"Here I am different. Here I'm..." She struggled for a way to explain herself, but could only manage the truth. "Here I'm me."

He seemed surprised by her candor, but then his expression softened. "Don't you know that *you* is who I want to make love to, Vivien? Unfettered by whatever masks you wear for others, uncontrolled by the rules you make for yourself. I wish to make love to *you*."

She could scarcely breathe as she swallowed past a suddenly thick throat. He was asking her for more than she had ever given anyone. From his expression, he recognized that fact, saw the seriousness of his request as he patiently waited for her to stop fighting this private war inside her and give him an answer to his appeal.

And the worst part was that deep inside, she wanted to say yes to this request. She wanted to give herself to him in a way she had never done before. To tell him the secrets he wanted to hear, the ones that could destroy her, because he would keep them safe.

But it wasn't fair to either of them to do that.

Was it?

She bit her lip with anxiety and avoided his stare as she whispered, "Not now. Not...yet."

He moved forward slightly. "But perhaps someday?"

She heard his hope and it both inspired a brief vision of a future she could never have and broke her heart.

And yet she did not refuse him. She couldn't, somehow, even if it was best for them both. She would leave soon, so the unnamed "someday" would never come. What harm would it do to leave that dream alive awhile longer, for both of them?

"Perhaps," she whispered. "But for now, why don't we go to the other chamber as we always have? There will be pleasure there, I promise you."

He cupped her chin and tilted it up to stare into her eyes. She shivered at how deeply he seemed to see. There was a connection there that terrified her. Thrilled her.

"There is always pleasure, Vivien," he said softly. "And one day I think there could be even more. If you let me in even a little."

She pulled back and moved to the door. She motioned him out, but as she followed him down the hallway toward the other bedchamber, she couldn't help but ponder the fact that his words mirrored Mariah's. Both encouraged her to allow someone past the walls she had built, into the heart she had long left cold and empty.

If only both of them could understand how impossible that request was.

He pushed the door open and briefly looked around at the false bedroom. She did the same and felt a curious emptiness that had never touched her before. There was nothing special about the big bed, the sensual lighting, the soft colors meant to seduce. There would be pleasure here tonight, but she feared she might regret not taking the other sensations Benedict had offered her a moment before.

Her regret softened, though, when he turned toward her, drew her to his chest and brought his mouth to hers in a kiss that melted her very bones with its heat and intention. She wrapped her arms around his neck, lifting herself against him as she prayed he would feel how much she did truly want and feel for him. That was all she could give him at the moment and it would have to be enough.

If he sensed the desperation behind her touch, he didn't speak of it, but merely guided her back to lie her across the bed. She watched as he slowly removed his clothing, tossing each item away until he stood totally and gloriously naked before her.

She leaned forward against her will, driven to touch him as if she had never touched a man before. She quivered with excitement, her body humming with a need to please him, taste him, claim him even if she never spoke words of love out loud.

Reaching out, she caught the smooth perfection of his cock in one palm, stroking him from base to tip. He let out a growl of pleasure, thrusting into her hand a second time as his cheeks flushed and cock hardened even more.

She licked her lips and then took him deep into her mouth, deep enough that he touched her throat and filled her entirely. She groaned at the sensation, how good it felt to give him this pleasure. It had always excited her to do so, and never with anyone more than him.

She pumped him deep within her mouth, rolling her tongue around him, feeling him twitch with pleasure he battled to control. She fought just as hard to steal that control as she added the gliding grip of her hand to her pleasuring.

He reached out and gripped the headrest, his eyes shut, and he moaned out her name low and sweet. His hips began to move in time to her strokes, maneuvering him closer and closer to exactly where she wanted him to be.

She smiled. Yes, she could still manipulate him when it came to sex. And that gave her some solace that her power remained.

But just as her smug satisfaction allowed her to relax, he tugged his cock from her lips and pushed her back to lie on the bed. He covered her body before she could protest and his mouth came down on hers with as much insistence and drive as she had exhibited a moment ago.

She melted into the kiss despite herself, lifting to be closer as he shoved her dress around her waist and covered her sex with his hand. He began to tease at her entrance, dragging his fingers across the weeping slit, just dipping their tips into the warmth there.

She gasped at the sensation and a sudden realization that flashed into her addled mind. This was a war. Both of them were battling for supremacy, control, surrender. In most relationships, those terms would be violent, but here they were about passion and emotion. She wanted only one, he demanded the other. She feared she was slipping, losing their battle, for feelings were creeping into her heart that gripped her with terror and regret.

She gasped as she shoved the thought away and instead opened her legs wider and lifted to force his fingertips inside her clenching sheath. He laughed.

"Always demanding," he whispered before he lowered himself over her, pinning her to the bed as he positioned his cock at her entrance.

Instead of taking her, though, he merely stared down at her, tenderly stroking her cheek.

"Don't you know, Vivien? You never have to demand from me. Simply ask for what you desire and I would give you anything." He kissed her. "Anything at all."

Unexpected tears leapt to her eyes as he slid deep within her in one slow stroke. She buried her face into his shoulder and lifted her hips to him, giving him with her body what she could not afford to share in her heart.

The electric explosion of orgasm hit her suddenly, without warning, so powerful that she screamed out against his flesh, digging her fingers into his back as wave after wave of pleasure crashed over her. He grunted in response and clutched her closer, his hips jerking erratically before she felt the hot splash of his seed inside her.

He went limp over her, cradling her to him as their panting breaths merged into one over seconds, moments. She clung to him, smoothing her hands over his back, pressing her lips to his flesh and knowing, more than she had ever known anything, that what she felt for him had gone too far.

She loved him. That fact was so clear that she couldn't believe she had ever doubted it. She loved him, just as she had loved him when they parted three years before. Just as she had loved him all throughout the interim of years that separated them.

And yet, even knowing that, she also knew that she could never have him. All the reasons that kept that from being possible still existed. Would always exist. So she would have to find a way to let him go, to cross him off her list, even though she would leave her heart with him in London when she finally swept out of the city for the last time.

CHAPTER 12

Vivien sat at her dressing table, staring at the list before her. Her list of unfinished business, which she had stuffed into a drawer when Benedict stumbled upon it three nights before. She hadn't dared to look at it since, knowing that she had not truly completed any of the items written on the heavy paper.

Knowing that certain items, like Benedict, would be left unfinished thanks to the foolish beating of her heart.

"Tonight I *shall* cross an item off," she said, looking at herself in the mirror.

Her appearance was the same, but how could that be? She was irrevocably changed now—how could it not be written all over her face?

"Foolish girl," she snapped as she got to her feet and smoothed her gown. "You will not become a ninny because of this man. Just because you feel something does not mean it will change you."

She stormed from the room and down the stairs to the parlor. She knew Mariah was waiting for her there and she refused to show her friend any difference in her demeanor.

Forcing a smile, she pushed the door open and stepped inside. Mariah was wearing a pretty gown, dark blue and covered in a fall of lighter flowers along the skirt. She looked…like a lady, which was, of course, what she was by marriage, but also by something deeper.

Suddenly Vivien felt quite out of place, even with her best friend.

"Oh, I do love that gown," Mariah gushed as she crossed the room to give her friend a quick squeeze.

Vivien looked down. Suddenly her green dress felt too low-cut, too revealing of both her body and who and what she was. Everyone would look at her, everyone would see…

"Thank you," she said, but her voice cracked.

Mariah stepped back to look at her closely. "What is it?"

"Am I so transparent?" Vivien asked on a sigh as she extracted herself from her friend's embrace and walked to the sideboard to pour herself a drink. "This does not bode well."

And it didn't. The last thing she wished to do was reveal too much of herself to the other guests at tonight's gathering or to Benedict, who was always looking for a revelation. She was teetering on a very dangerous edge now. She couldn't afford to fall.

"I do not think I've ever seen you so flustered," Mariah said, taking a seat on the settee and motioning her over to join her.

Reluctantly, Vivien did so and allowed Mariah to take both her hands.

"What is it?" her friend encouraged.

Vivien had spent a lifetime pretending away her thoughts and feelings, pushing them aside so no one would see. Tonight, she found she had no energy to do so.

"I do not belong at this party," she whispered as hot blood rushed to her cheeks.

Mariah tilted her head and there was true surprise on her face. "My dearest, you are nervous. I had no idea. But you have been to many a public gathering with lovers in the past."

Vivien bit her lip. "There is a great deal of difference between a small gathering at a home of a lover or his friend, or even the opera or the theatre, and a soiree like this one."

Mariah smiled. "Yes, there is. But again, you have come to these sorts of things before, and your friends who are mistresses have attended them with your specific orders to keep their chins up and proud. What makes it different that you are so anxious now?"

Vivien swallowed and turned away, not wanting Mariah to see what she feared she couldn't keep from her face. She drew a few breaths to calm herself, to formulate some kind of answer that would diffuse her friend's curiosity before she delved too deep. But it was all too late. Mariah leaned back.

"It is because of Benedict Greystone, isn't it?" she whispered.

Vivien squeezed her eyes shut. "No, of course not."

But there was no strength to her refusal and Mariah was too clever not to know that. Her face crumpled with pity and understanding.

"He asked you to attend tonight, Vivien. He is not ashamed and neither should you be. He wants you there."

Vivien nodded slowly. He did want her there, and not only because they would enact their plans against Dersingham tonight.

"I'm certain his brother will be none too pleased to see me, though," Vivien said with an empty laugh as she got up and paced to the fire.

"And since when do you care what a lover's family thinks?" Mariah chuckled.

Vivien bit her lip. It was a valid question. But she did care, and always had. Hell, it was partly because of the Earl of Abbotton that she had parted ways from Benedict before. Not that he knew that. Nor would he ever know it.

"Are you in love with Benedict Greystone?" Mariah suddenly asked.

Vivien turned on her. Her friend had not moved from her place on the settee, but there was tension in her stare and a knowing in her eyes that unsettled Vivien. Was the truth so patently clear? Or had Mariah just managed to get close enough to see it?

And how to respond? Part of her wanted to admit the truth, to admit everything, including how she had decided to leave London, that she was pursuing this list of loose ends, that she didn't know what to do. If she confessed all, Mariah would be sympathetic and helpful. Her friend would do anything and everything in her power to assist.

And yet, as she opened her mouth, Vivien found she could not do it. She couldn't reveal herself, not even to her friend. The weight of her loneliness crushed her as she said, "Of course not. Don't be foolish."

Mariah hesitated, then shrugged one shoulder. "Very well. But I hope you know that—"

Vivien bit her lip. Mariah was going to keep pushing. "Oh, look at the time," she interrupted, glancing at the clock on the mantel. "We have chattered too long. We should depart now."

Mariah stared, but then slowly got to her feet and nodded. She turned toward the foyer. Vivien nodded as she followed Mariah out to her carriage.

Mariah's husband had been out of London on business for two days and they would reunite at the ball tonight. And since Vivien hadn't wanted to share a carriage with Benedict thanks to her raw emotions, she had agreed to ride with her friend instead and meet him there.

But as she stepped into the vehicle and settled across from Mariah, Vivien couldn't help but think that somehow this was all a terrible mistake. That she would come to regret this night. But the carriage was already moving and it was too late to turn back.

Benedict glanced down yet again and soaked in the image of Vivien on his arm. This was everything he had ever imagined in troubling dreams over the past few years.

She shifted and glanced up at him. Through clenched teeth, she managed, "They are all *looking* at me."

Benedict looked into the crowd. Most were very content to talk to their friends, but a few extra glances were being spared his way. The gentlemen had knowing in those glances, which was not unexpected. Most did have an awareness of who Vivien was. The women seemed to look for *another* reason.

"I believe they may be looking at me, not you," he said with as much reassurance as he could put in his tone since she seemed unexpectedly uncomfortable.

She blinked. "Because you are on the market?"

He nodded and just held back a sigh at the thought. His mother, who was not in attendance tonight thanks to a prior engagement, had been working at a massive rate to ensure every chaperone and debutante knew that he was on the lookout for a bride sooner rather than later. The result was all these appraising stares.

"So even though you are with a mystery woman, they would still pursue you?"

He glanced at her again. Her tone and face were both perturbed. "Jealous?" he asked.

She jerked her face toward him, but before she could answer, she looked past him and squeezed his arm. "*There* is your American," she whispered.

He glanced over his shoulder and found that Felicity Beecher and her father were indeed coming across the ballroom together.

"Excellent, then the game begins," Benedict said and maneuvered them into the path of the pair. He felt Vivien tense as the pair stopped.

"Ah, Mr. Beecher," Benedict said with a slight bow to the gentleman and his daughter. "And Miss Felicity. I did not know you two would be in attendance tonight."

Beecher eyed him in the same way all chaperones did now—with interest, even though this man intended his daughter for someone else. But Beecher wanted a title, which Benedict did not and would never have, so he felt quite safe in the other man's analysis.

"Mr. Greystone," Beecher finally said with a slight smile. "I have not seen you since that gathering at Rockholm Center a few weeks ago."

"Quite a boring fete," Benedict laughed and it was genuine.

"I certainly thought so," Felicity interjected with a bright smile for him. Then her gaze flitted to Vivien. "I'm sorry, we haven't met."

Benedict jolted as if he had all but forgotten his companion. "Great God, my manners. This is Miss Vivien, a friend of mine."

"Very pleased to make your acquaintance, Mr. Beecher, Miss Felicity." Vivien's tone seemed strained as she extended a hand, but Benedict assumed this was because of their plan.

Benedict leaned a fraction closer to Beecher as Vivien made vague small talk with Felicity.

"I have heard that there are congratulations in order."

Beecher arched a brow. "Congratulations?"

Benedict grinned. "Come now, do not be coy. It is common knowledge that your daughter has matched with the Earl of Dersingham's son. I believe he is currently Viscount Topperly?"

Beecher smiled slightly. "Ah, word does get around in a Society such as this. We have not announced the engagement yet, but yes, we intend to do so tonight."

Right on cue, Vivien turned from Felicity with a laugh. "Oh, did I hear you say Topperly?"

Beecher glanced at her with uncertainty and Benedict almost had to laugh. Americans who were hurtled into their realm were almost always staggered by the connections of their Society. At this moment, the poor man was probably trying to figure out exactly who and what Vivien was. In a moment, he would know.

"Yes, indeed I did," Beecher said with a quick glance around due to the loudness with which Vivien had asked the question.

"Good old Tops," Vivien said with a sentimental sigh. "Most men aren't like him."

"What do you mean?" Felicity asked slowly and her stare was quickly becoming concerned.

Vivien leaned toward her father instead. "You needn't worry

about him, sir. The man has taken very good care of his other families. I'm certain he will take care of the one he creates with your daughter."

Both the Beechers gasped in unison and Felicity took a step away from Vivien like she had suddenly become poison. Benedict stifled a smile. This was perfect.

"Oh dear," Vivien said with a glance up toward Benedict. "I thought they knew…"

Benedict patted her hand. "My dear, we do not usually speak of such delicate topics at events such as these."

Vivien's expression of embarrassment was so true that even Benedict almost believed it. "Oh my," she said, her tone strained. "I do apologize!"

Beecher was sputtering, maneuvering his daughter away from them as he stared at Vivien almost as if she had sprouted a second head. "I—I…good evening!"

With that, he grabbed his daughter and dragged her away. Benedict grinned after them. "Now he will go to some friend he trusts and ask about what you've said."

Vivien nodded slowly. "And I'm certain said friend will tell them exactly who and what I am, which will lend credence to my accusations."

Benedict glanced at her. Her tone was very flat, but her face revealed nothing.

"Indeed, it will," he reassured her. "The damage is done. I hope you are happy about that."

She lifted her face to his, examining him closely, but she didn't have a chance to speak because at that moment another person spoke. From behind him, Benedict heard his name. And when he turned, he found his brother and his brother's wife standing there, staring at him…staring at her.

The tension in her hand against his arm tightened and for a moment her face revealed pure terror. Benedict had no understanding of why. She had met his brother a few times during their first affair, but why she felt so strongly about him, Benedict did not know.

"Lord and Lady Abbotton," he drawled with a smile that challenged his brother to say something about his companion. "I did not realize you two would be in attendance tonight."

Derek arched a brow. "I imagine you did not."

Benedict ignored the judgmental tone of his brother's answer and turned his attention toward Jocelyn. His sister-in-law kept casting side glances at Vivien but had not yet acknowledged her. Nor had his brother.

"Jocelyn, you look lovely."

She smiled, but the version of it was weak indeed. "Thank you, Benedict."

"And I do not think you have met my companion—" he began.

His brother moved forward slightly, almost as if to protect Jocelyn. "My wife knows who she is."

Vivien sucked in a breath but did not move nor allow her reaction to be present on her face.

Derek turned to her. "Vivien," he said, the barest of welcomes said on the barest of polite tones.

She swallowed. "Lord Abbotton." She glanced at his wife with a shaky smile. "And Lady Abbotton, congratulations on your marriage."

Jocelyn nodded, but there was stiff discomfort and confusion about what to do on her face. Benedict couldn't understand it. He knew her to be a kind woman, friendly to all, and yet she could scarcely look at Vivien.

There was a moment of the awkwardness that stretched between them for what seemed like an eternity and then Vivien broke it in the most unusual way possible.

She turned to Benedict. "I am afraid I find myself with a headache. Thank you for including me tonight, but I think I shall return home."

Benedict stared at her. She was running? "Vivien—"

She held up a hand and faced his brother and sister-in-law with false brightness. "It is always a pleasure to see you. Do enjoy your evening."

His brother seemed to feel no pleasure as he bid her farewell and watched her turn to depart the ballroom. His face was grim.

Benedict couldn't help it, he rushed to follow her, proving to himself yet again that he was bound to this woman in ways he could hardly explain. Ways she did not desire.

There seemed to be no escaping that fact, no matter what he did.

CHAPTER 13

Vivien could scarcely breathe as she made her way across the ballroom. It felt like every eye followed her, disgusted expressions greeted her, the walls closed in on her and she could barely contain an urge to run toward the carriage she knew awaited her on the drive.

Guests were still entering the ballroom as she burst into the cool night air and looked for her driver in the fray of servants and party-goers. Suddenly a servant for the house was at her elbow, looking at her benignly.

"May I assist, miss?"

She nodded. "I am looking for my friend's driver, I must depart immediately."

The servant did not register a reaction to this statement, despite the early hour, but merely took her information and set off to find the man in the collection of servants who had taken their masters' vehicles behind the house to wait for the party's end many hours from now.

She shifted in the night air, moving off into the shadow of the house so the latecomers would not see her. How she wished *no one* could see her after tonight.

But that was not to be, for at that moment the man who saw her most clearly stepped outside, scanning for her.

Benedict.

She stared at him in the fraction of a moment before he saw her. He looked so handsome in his formal attire. So much above her in a way she often tried to pretend wasn't true. Tonight had proven it, yet again.

"There you are," he said as he caught sight of her in the shadows. She held her breath as he approached, hoping she would not reveal too much of herself. "What is wrong?"

She shrugged one shoulder and wished the servant would hurry so that Mariah's carriage would come and save her. "As I said, it is a headache, nothing more. Please do not trouble yourself about it."

He stared at her. "Vivien," he whispered. "I do not believe that is all there is to this sudden desire to depart. What is wrong?"

She hesitated. There was no use in pretending if he would not accept that. She sighed. "Benedict, I ask you to please accept my excuse. Let me go."

He stared at her for a moment and then he reached out to take her hand. They were both wearing gloves, but his fingers warmed her regardless. They made her want to lean into him and allow for this comfort he wished to offer. It was only her long years of practicing control that kept her from doing something so foolish.

"Benedict," she whispered. "I do not belong here. Tonight has reminded me of that fact."

He shook his head. "That isn't true."

"It is," she said, with more force and volume than perhaps she had intended. "You saw Beecher's reaction. He and Felicity were horrified when I spoke, when they began to suspect what I was."

"That was our intention, wasn't it?" Benedict asked.

She frowned. "It was, yes. But that does not make it any more pleasant. And your brother and his wife…"

He shook his head. "He was cold to you, I know. And I don't know why she was so standoffish—she is usually very kind."

For the first time since the night began, she smiled, soft and indulgent. "Come, Benedict, do not be naïve. You know exactly why they behaved as they did. Your sister-in-law is a *lady*. I am most definitely not. She should not be kind to me, nor welcoming. She has been taught her whole life that women like me are a plague, one she might even believe is transmittable by touch or kindness. No, the fact that she even acknowledged my existence at all is a boon, and I know it."

He stared at her, shaking his head, and she could see there was a part of him that knew what she said was true and it warred with a part that still didn't want to believe that their lives could be so disparate. That there could be no chance of these worlds being able to merge.

He still loved her. And the fact of it stung like fire.

She backed away, releasing his hand even though she did not want to do it. "Benedict, go back inside. There are women there who will want to be what you need."

He shook his head. "I see none of them."

"Then let me help you. Miss Felicity herself was very much interested in you." Saying the words was as difficult as seeing the evidence had been earlier. "She is smitten. Perhaps you can do something to encourage that."

"I don't—" he began again, but she did not allow it.

"Stop. Embrace the life you are meant to live."

He gritted his teeth, his frustration clear on his face. "That isn't what I want."

Vivien all but collapsed with relief as she saw the carriage finally circling around in the drive toward her. She stepped toward it.

"Please, let me go," she whispered, motioning the driver down to open her door. "It's best for us both."

She didn't wait for his reply, but simply got into her carriage. As the driver closed the door and clambered back on top, she dared to look at Benedict out the window. Never before had she seen such a forlorn expression on a man and it made her want to fling herself from the carriage and into his arms. Even if it wasn't the right thing to do. Even if it would hurt them both in the end.

Luckily, the driver had no idea of her desire and the vehicle began to move before she could do something so foolish. Instead, she sank back against the leather seats and tried to remind herself that tonight she had crossed off something from her list.

That would have to be enough.

~

Benedict reentered the ballroom without seeing anything around him anymore. The din of the crowd faded to the background as he reached for a drink from a passing tray. He wanted to drown himself in something, anything, to make himself forget Vivien's face as she drove away, leaving him behind. She had seemed...*empty*, something he had never seen in her before.

Worse was the fact that *he* had done that. Using her reputation to work against Dersingham had hurt her. He had never guessed that would be the case. After all, she had been the one to suggest how they bring her character into the discussion, and yet it was clear that being perceived as a lesser person...by Beecher, by his own brother...it cut her to the quick. It made her want to hide.

Why hadn't he thought of that? Why had he only pictured her as the tough courtesan who never let anything past her façade. He'd always known there was more to her.

He downed the drink in one slug and was ready to look for another when he felt a hard tap on his shoulder. He turned to find Derek standing there, Jocelyn at his side. His brother looked frustrated. No, angry.

"Are you trying to destroy yourself?" Derek snapped, keeping his tone low even though the emotion in it was clear.

"Oh, bugger off," Benedict retorted with an apologetic look to the utterly scandalized Jocelyn. "What do you know about it?"

"You brought a..." He sent his own contrite look toward his wife.

"A *whore* here to a public event when you are supposed to be in the process of seeking a bride. Do you not think that will cause you problems?"

Benedict moved on his brother. "Call her a whore again and I will make you pay for it."

Derek blinked at him, his expression a combination of pity, disgust and anger. "She is what she is. If you asked her, I wager she would be blunt enough to tell you the same. Vivien Manning has always been a straightforward type, something I actually appreciate about her."

"But little else," Benedict growled. "Which is why you and your wife were so cold to her."

Derek stared at him, stunned silent by his words. The look went on for so long that Benedict began to feel awkward beneath the regard. Intruded upon.

"I need air," his brother finally said, his voice raw and rough. "Jocelyn?"

But to Benedict's surprise, his sister-in-law shook her head. "You go. I will join you shortly."

His brother hesitated, then jerked out a nod and stormed off across the room toward the veranda doors in the distance. Benedict just barely stifled a curse and sent a quick glance toward Jocelyn.

"I apologize for our bickering," he said softly. "You do not deserve to be in the middle of such things."

She smiled sadly. "I am going to be in the middle of them for some time, you know. Family squabbles are to be expected from time to time." She moved a little closer. "Your brother only wants what is best for you."

"Yes, and of course he knows what that is, better than I do myself," Benedict grunted.

She tilted her head. "He believes he does, I'm certain of that."

"Well, it is easy for him to judge," he said on a sigh as his frustration began to fade in the face of her gentleness. "He has love."

Jocelyn stepped back, her eyes widening. "You love this woman?"

Benedict pursed his lips. He had not meant to say it out loud, but there was no denying it now that it had been said. He had always loved Vivien. Sadly, he feared he always would.

"I do," he admitted, watching her closely to see her reaction.

She had been so put off by Vivien a short time ago, not that his lover seemed to blame her for that. But now her expression became less uncomfortable, more questioning than judging.

"Forgive me, I am quite unsophisticated when it comes to these matters," Jocelyn said slowly. "I have always been taught that men did not have those kinds of feelings for people like…like her."

"What does that mean?" he asked, trying to keep himself from being too unkind and harsh when her choice of terms irked him. *"People like her*? What kind of a person is she?"

Jocelyn shook her head. "Benedict, your tone is unforgiving, but you must acknowledge that a lady such as myself, a lady like most in this room, has been sheltered from the kind of society a person like Vivien Manning keeps. I am not trying to slur against her, but to do my best to label what I don't understand."

Benedict bent his head. "I'm sorry. I did not mean to take my frustrations out on you when they should be aimed at myself. You see, I hurt Vivien tonight by using the very reputation, the very shock of her presence that you describe."

Her brow wrinkled. "To what end?"

He hesitated. That was far too complicated an answer. "To help her do something she asked of me. But I should have been more sensitive."

"Are you certain you were not also using her to keep yourself from finding the bride that your family desires?" his sister-in-law asked softly.

He looked at her. The girl might be innocent in many ways, but not naïve. She clearly saw more than he had given her credit for.

"I do not deny that the side effect of that would not be unwelcome."

She nodded. "Then I see how she could be hurt by it. No matter her character."

"But you do not see that her character is not the same as her reputation," he explained, wishing he could make *someone* in his life see what a vibrant and wonderful being Vivien was. "She has walked a path very different from your own, yes, and I must tell you that it has not always been by choice. But she has a heart. She has dreams. She has everything inside her that any woman hopes for."

Jocelyn nodded slowly. "I suppose I had not ever considered that."

He shrugged. "No one in our Society ever does, it seems. I think even she sometimes believes she isn't the same kind of person as anyone else. That somehow she has been inherently damaged by her past."

"I imagine that must be painful to her. And to you since you say you love her." She said the words slowly and though Benedict could see he had reached her in some way, she remained shocked by it all.

He shook his head. "You needn't worry about how her existence will affect yours, you know. Vivien makes it clear on a regular basis that she will never accept my love. My plans for the future remain unchanged. I will do what is 'right' and will be accepted by my brother and my family."

Saying those words made his stomach turn. Yet he had no choice. To his surprise, Jocelyn did not look relieved by this declaration, but pained.

"Benedict," she said softly.

He shook his head. "I have troubled you enough with these thoughts. You should go find my brother and enjoy what is left of your evening."

"But—" she began.

"Please don't worry yourself," he interrupted with a false smile. "In the end, there is nothing any of us can do to change the circumstance. It isn't your duty to burden yourself with my problems."

She nodded, too slowly for him to believe she could wipe this discussion from her mind. Then she looked off toward the veranda and did as he asked by weaving into the crowd to seek out her husband.

He cursed as he took a second drink. Tonight had been an utter disaster when he had hoped it would serve as proof that he and Vivien could create a powerful partnership. Tomorrow he would have to work to salvage whatever he could…if she would even allow him that chance.

CHAPTER 14

Vivien looked out her carriage window and was dragged back to the previous night, when her final image from a very similar window had been of Benedict staring after her as she left him behind after the ball. She had dreamed of that moment all night, waking up sweating as thoughts of him tortured her instead of allowing her restful sleep.

She opened her reticule and pulled from it the list of loose ends in order to remove her mind from that other, far more unpleasant subject. Today she had other things in mind than dwelling on what she could not have.

No, today was about continuing to move forward in the future. Despite the fact that it had ended badly, last night she had done what she had set out to do. Her spies had reported that Beecher had refused to announce the engagement to Dersingham's son and had actually broken the engagement right in one of the parlors at the gathering, much to Dersingham's public humiliation. If Benedict was correct in his assessment of Dersingham's finances, he was currently on the path to destitution.

Crossing off her duty to "destroy someone evil" was very satisfying indeed.

And today she would complete another task, as well as give herself a stern reminder about how to control her heart. The carriage stopped and she reached over to fetch the small parcel she had brought along with her. As the door opened, she smiled at her driver.

"Thank you, Greenley. I should be at least an hour if you would like to visit your sister at the Warren residence. It is only a few doors down, is it not?"

He smiled. "Yes, miss. Thank you, miss. I'll get the carriage situated and I will take a walk down there as you suggest."

She patted his hand, then moved up to the house she had once known so very well. The first time she visited here, she had been terrified, but it had eventually become a safe *home* for her. The first one she'd ever really known.

The door opened before she could knock and she was led to a parlor by a cheery housemaid. The place had been redone since her time here. The walls had been repapered and the furniture was fresh and new. Time marched on, no matter what.

A fact proven even further when the door to the parlor opened and the Duke of Sandcombe entered. It had been only ten years since their affiliation, but he had aged twice that number of years since. Illness made him thin, grayed his hair, stooped his back. Tears flooded her eyes at the sight, but she blinked them back, knowing he would not wish for, nor appreciate her pity.

"Walter," she said, her voice bright as she moved to kiss both his cheeks.

She slipped her arm through his and used the motion to help him to a seat without making too much of a fuss about it. He smiled up at her as he settled into his place.

"An old trick, girlie. I see you're trying to fuss over me."

She laughed as she retook her seat across from him. "I cannot help it. Long-held habits are hard to break."

"Yes. You always did take good care of me. It was a blessing," he said, his tone suddenly far away.

Vivien shifted under the uncomfortable weight of memory and emotion. She grabbed for the parcel she had brought with her and held it out to him.

"Your favorites."

His eyes twinkled as he pulled away the ribbon and layer of thin paper to reveal a box of truffles imported by Niles Chocolatier from a chocolate shop in Switzerland.

"The only chocolates Niles does not make in his own shop, though how he imports them when the Swiss are part of Napoleon's regime is beyond me," she said as Walter pulled the box top away and ate one of the sweets with an expression of bliss.

He held the box out, but she shook her head. He put the box on a table at his side and settled back to stare at her. "I cannot believe you have only come here to bring me chocolate and talk to me about import and export of the same. Though I could probably tell you a bit about it."

"You think I have an ulterior motive for my appearance here?" she asked. "No, I have only been thinking about you of late. You taught me very valuable lessons during your time as my protector."

He tilted his head as if he did not understand where she was going with the conversation. A point of pride for her, since normally Walter was seven steps ahead of anyone who played a game of verbal chess with him.

"What lessons did you learn at my feet, dear Vivien?"

"You were my first protector," she explained, pushing to her feet as she suddenly felt quite restless. "You taught me how to hold myself when I was on your arm, how to be polite and comfortable in all parts of Society, low or high, and what to say in every situation."

He waved his hand. "Any protector could have taught you those things. You were eager and quick to learn."

She didn't look at him, but out the window as she pondered that. "I suppose any protector could have done this, but most wouldn't have wasted the time. They would have kept me as a whore, not a mistress. Or they would have decided I was not worth the trouble."

He shrugged one shoulder. "You were beautiful and talented in the ways of your path. You would have been worth the trouble to anyone with a brain."

She smiled at his attempts to soften what she knew to be true. This man had saved her when most others would not have. She owed him a boon even if he played it off as nothing.

"There was one more lesson you taught me."

He smiled. "What is that? How to lace your shoes?"

She laughed, though she was utterly serious when she whispered, "You taught me how to keep my heart separate from the feelings of my body."

"Ah." He pursed his lips together as his smile faded. "*Those* lessons. I suppose they were a good thing. In theory."

She tilted her head. Walter had always been firm on the fact that one should never allow a lover too far into one's heart. Now he wavered on the same notion?

"What do you mean?"

He fingered a loose thread on the settee, drawing her attention to the worn fabric. It was different than it had been during her last visit, but she could see now it was not of better quality.

He sighed. "I suppose I mean that as I grow older and closer to death—"

She caught her breath. "No!"

He arched a brow. "Don't be foolish, girl. Look at me. I'm a shadow of my former self. Death will visit in the next few years, I wager."

She said nothing, for she could not deny the terrible toll life had taken on him. Nor the consequence of the death he now expected.

"And now that I have reached the end of my life," he continued. "I sometimes regret separating my heart from my body. It cost me friends, lovers, even my own children, who do not call on me except when it is required." He sighed softly. "Loneliness is a difficult pill to swallow, even if it is entirely of one's own making."

"Yes," Vivien found herself whispering and caught her breath as she heard the word in her own voice. "Not that I am lonely."

"Even during the nights where you do not fill your home with partygoers and lovers?" he asked, his tone and expression benign for such a volatile question.

She hesitated. "I suppose those nights are long," she admitted. "But I fill them with my own pursuits."

"Reading, sewing, conversation with friends, I know what you mean. And I suppose there are rewards in those things." He shook his head. "But there is nothing like the love of a partner. Someone who is not obligated to care for you because of blood ties or financial ones."

He frowned and she saw a line of loss across his face that brought tears to her eyes a second time. She blinked them away again, but felt sorrow remain. For him. For herself. In twenty years, thirty years, forty years...she would face the same end as her old friend now did. Isolated in another country, she would rely on casual acquaintances and paid help to send her off to her final rest.

Not Benedict. Not her children.

"You are still young," Walter's voice broke into her painful thoughts and forced her to remember that she stood in his parlor. She had floated away for a moment. "I hope you might still leave room for love, despite what I taught you."

"And what if that love cannot last?" she asked, thinking of the stares of Benedict's friends, the dismissive tone of his brother and the shock of his sister-in-law.

He shrugged. "Even if it cannot, the memories will fill some of the emptiness when it is gone, will it not?"

She jolted at the thought. She'd always considered the memories associated with love as potentially painful, but she could also see how they might be a comfort. Any moment she shared with Benedict was one she could live over in her mind, replaying like a story where she was the heroine of the piece.

She had a great deal more to think about than she had imagined when she came here hoping Walter could straighten her head. Instead, she was more jumbled and confused than ever.

She shook her head. There were other reasons she had come and now she could use those to change this tender subject, at least until she had had enough time to consider it further.

"You know, this is not why I have come here either," she said.

He cocked his head. "Always protecting yourself from delicate subjects. Then why did you come if not to hear me wax poetic on the benefits of emotion?"

She shifted. "I have heard you have perhaps had some hardship beyond your illness," she said, pressing into this very delicate subject with the greatest of care. Walter had been a proud man when they were together.

To her surprise, he chuckled at her question rather than avoid it. "You are referring, I suppose, to my disastrous loss of fortune?"

She hesitated and then nodded slightly. "If you wish to tell me about it."

He waved a hand as if it were meaningless. "The money that was not bound up in entail was drained away by empty endeavors and poor investments. Since I turned over all the estate business to my son, a bit of balm on the wounds I caused all those years ago, it is coming back. But my home here and my lifestyle are greatly reduced, I admit."

Vivien nodded. "I owe you a debt, Walter."

He lifted both eyebrows as her statement sank in. "No."

"Yes," she said, with as much strength as his denial. "I would have been on the street if it had not been for your assistance all those years ago. You took your reputation and placed it over me, making me a commodity other men desired. And you settled me well enough that it began my rise. So I owe you this."

He stared at her. "Why? Why now?"

She pondered how to respond and decided the truth was the best way. "Walter, I am leaving London. This Season shall be my last."

She wobbled a little on her feet. Since making her grand announcement to her servant a few weeks before, she had not spoken her decision out loud. Now she heard the words, felt their finality, and it staggered her.

It seemed to do the same for him. He blinked at her, face blank as if he hadn't understood the language she spoke. After what seemed like an eternity, he said, "I beg your pardon."

"I am going to go to the continent and start over. Buy a little home, create a new name. I'll call myself a rich widow and have a different life." She sighed. "But there are things left to do here. Words to be said. And people, like you, to thank."

He reached out a hand and she rushed to him, taking it as she settled in next to him.

"Vivien," he murmured.

She smiled. There was so much to just her name. So much understanding that passed between them. She squeezed his fingers gently. "I'm going to deposit a sum in an account for you."

He jolted. "No, Vivien, truly—"

"Tush," she interrupted as she slipped her hand from his. "Allow me to settle my debt with you and cross it from my ledger."

"You owe me no debt," he insisted, but his tone grew weaker with every word.

She leaned across and gently kissed his cheek. "I wish to repay it, regardless. Hire a pretty nurse with it. Let her take care of you...in more ways than one."

He burst into laughter that put the youth back into his eyes. "When you put it that way, how could I refuse?"

She pushed to her feet. "Excellent. I will send word to you this afternoon once the deed has been done."

He watched her but did not stand, proof yet again of his weakened state. "Will you see me again before you go?"

She nodded. "I will. Now do not trouble yourself by seeing me out. I can do that myself. I'll let your servant know."

He smiled his goodbye and she slipped from the room and from his home with only a few words. Outside, Greenley had returned from his own visit and was standing beside her vehicle with a satisfied smile.

"I trust your sister is well?" she asked as he helped her into the carriage.

He nodded. "Oh yes, ma'am. Right as rain. I hope your visit was just as pleasant."

She smiled and he stepped away. As soon as he was gone, her smile faded. Seeing her old friend had been a bittersweet pill indeed. And his remarks on love left her spinning.

But the more she pondered them, the more she wondered— could she dare to allow her heart to rule her, even for a few weeks? Would she be able to survive on those memories for years to come? Did she have the nerve to do it and know that the pain at her parting from Benedict would be far greater than anything she had ever known?

CHAPTER 15

The latest party his mother had dragged him to had been a failure of nightmarish proportions and Benedict's head pounded as he entered his foyer. He waved off his chattering butler and trudged up the stairs.

His mother knew about Vivien. She wasn't so indelicate as to state her knowledge outright, thank God, but her desperation in matchmaking and her comments about appropriate brides made it clear that his brother had taken his concerns to a whole new level.

Now debutantes were being thrown at him like tomatoes at a street skirmish and because of his attachment to title and his ownership of no small fortune, not a one seemed to care about Vivien's appearance at the earlier party. He had danced until he was certain he had a blister and the empty, cloying chattering of chaperones echoed in his mind.

He pushed open his chamber door and slammed it behind him with the heel of his boot. Boots he immediately began to remove even as he made for the bell to call for his valet. Before he could do so, a voice stopped him.

"I would be happy to stand in Mr. Aubrey's stead if you are in need of assistance."

His hand still hung in the air, inches from the bell, and he could not bring himself to turn right away for fear he would find the room empty.

"Benedict?" the voice repeated.

He finally forced himself to move toward that voice and sighed with relief as he saw Vivien standing beside his bed, watching him. Her blonde hair was down around her shoulders and back, her dress had been removed at some point and she was wearing a thin, silky white negligee in its place. In the firelight, her body was perfectly outlined beneath it.

He swallowed past a suddenly thick throat.

"I did not expect to see you here," he whispered.

She moved a step closer. "I hope that doesn't mean I'm not welcome."

He shook his head. "Most welcome, I assure you."

She slipped closer, but he held out a hand. "I need to say something. I know I hurt you at the ball the other night. When you did not return my missive the next day, I believed you wished to end our affair. Not that I blamed you."

She held out a hand to him. "Oh, Benedict, firstly it was *I* who thought up the idea of how to handle Beecher that night, to trade on my less-than-stellar reputation. I had no right to be affronted by what my own words wrought. It was churlish to do so. And the reason I did not reply to your missive *was* because I pondered ending our affair, for your good as much as mine."

"You did?" He stared, confused by her openness, as much as her presence. "And yet you are here despite your thoughts about ending our affair. Unless I am dreaming."

She laughed. "You are not dreaming lest it is a shared dream between us. I am here because what is between us has always been so much more complicated than I have ever admitted. Leaving, breaking from you...it has never been as easy for me as it should have been."

He drew back. In the years they'd known each other, that was the closest thing to a confession of emotion he'd ever heard.

"I'm not ready to be parted from you again," she whispered as she lifted his hand to her breast. "So please don't ask me any more questions. Let us leave analysis for another day. Just be with me, here, tonight."

If he had protests or further inquiries about her decisions, they melted from his mind as he slipped his free hand into her hair, tilted her face and pressed his lips to her. Being with her was the one thing he knew how to do. If she desired pleasure, he could most definitely do that for her...with great satisfaction.

His opposite hand, which she had placed on her breast, began to move, gliding the back of it up and down, brushing the nipple through the thin fabric of her nightrail until she shivered against his lips and made a sound of pleasure deep in her throat. She slid her hand up his chest, past his shoulder and draped it over the back of his neck as she lifted herself in eagerness to be closer.

He guided her to his bed and when he laid her against the pillows, he looked down at her. Closer was always what they had fought to be, at least in bed. Even when she pushed him aside emotionally, she had opened her arms to him physically.

Perhaps it was her only way of accepting him. Perhaps that was the only way he could soothe her fears and make her feel safe and loved.

He dropped his lips to hers a second time, but this time the kiss was gentled. He stroke his tongue over hers, tasting her slowly, savoring every second that he was so close. He felt her relax with his ministrations, which was in itself a movement of trust. One he intended to prove he was worthy of.

He pulled back and moved to his side, cuddled close to her. He fingered the lacy strap of her night rail. "This is beautiful."

She looked up at him and her surprise was evident. "Thank you. I had it made years ago, but never wore it."

"Never?" he repeated in surprise.

The corner of her lip quirked up. "No one else would have appreciated it as much as you."

"I doubt that, but I encourage it if only so that I will be the only man ever to see you in it." He leaned over her to press a kiss against the front of her shoulder, around the strap he had been fingering.

She let out a little sigh. "That is very nice."

"Indeed," he agreed, his breath coming short as he kissed lower, where the strap connected to the gown itself. "As is that."

He pushed the strap from her shoulder and revealed the smooth globe of her breast. They were the perfect breasts, really. Sized just to fit into his hands, rounded and peaked with dark, dusky-rose nipples that currently strained and were hardened by desire.

"I have always been fascinated by your breasts," he said as he flicked his thumb over the peak once, twice.

She shivered, but laughed. "My breasts or breasts in general?"

He glanced up at her with a playfully stern expression. "Both, I suppose, but mostly yours. Their sensitivity has long been a study of mine."

To accentuate the words, he leaned over and stroked his tongue over the nipple, swirling it in a tight circle around the peak while Vivien cried out with pleasure that made him laugh against her skin.

"You see, my research is proven," he teased, returning his attention to lightly thumbing the now-wet nipple.

"I can see that I must abandon myself to this, for it is quite important work," she said, her tone playful but strained by desire. "The ramifications could be far reaching."

He chuckled, loving this lightness between them. "Indeed. All womankind could benefit from your brave bearing of my experiments."

"Then experiment away," she breathed.

She smiled up at him and his breath caught. Had she ever been so lovely? Relaxed and playful, he could see something girlish in her. Something she hid from the world behind that façade of the knowing, experienced mistress to the important and rich. Tonight he truly was with someone no other man had seen or touched, a fact that gave him great pleasure.

He shook his head to clear those thoughts and while he continued to tease her nipple with one hand, he glided the other down the long, silky length of her nightgown until he caught the hem. He began to hike the dress up, past her knees, her thighs, until he rested a swath of white satin against her stomach.

"I thought your research was dedicated to my breasts?" she asked, staring down the length of her body to his hand, which now rested on her smooth, naked thigh. "Or have you moved on to a new subject?"

"Indeed not," he said, pretending affront at such a suggestion. "But my most interesting point of study is how connected they are to your ultimate pleasure. For instance, when I do this…"

He sucked her naked nipple between his lips and began to suckle, tugging hard on the engorged flesh. Vivien gasped and then began to writhe, gripping at the coverlet, lifting her hips as she moaned out a sound of pure pleasure.

"Ah, you see," he said, letting her nipple slide from his lips with a pop. He glided his fingers up until he lightly fingered her sex. "Very wet now. I can make a conclusion."

She was out of breath, staring at him with wide, wild eyes. "And that is?" she panted.

"Making you writhe is one of the greatest pleasures of my life," he responded as he moved his lips over hers.

Although he had been playful, it was evident he had truly brought her to a point of pleasure that bordered on madness. She wrapped her arms around his neck and dragged him against her with all her might, her kiss wild and passionate, drugging and seductive.

As much as he wanted to savor this moment, to play with her, tease her, he couldn't deny that his body ached for more fulfilling games. He wanted to be inside her, joined with her in the most primal way possible. He wanted to feel the wet stroke of her sheath as he drove deep within her. He wanted to make the tremors of her release build until her body milked the same from his.

He pulled back and stared down at her. Her bright eyes held his and for a moment he saw every emotion she so skillfully hid every day. He saw desire, yes, but also fear and sadness, loss and yearning, and even a flicker of love, bright but gone before he could verify it had existed.

"Please," she whispered.

He couldn't deny her request. Gently, he tugged her gown over her other shoulder and dragged the entire contraption away from her body. He tossed the silk over the edge of the bed and looked at her, naked and perfect against his pillows. Tonight she was his and he intended to take full advantage of that.

He returned his attention to her breasts, pressing them together so that he could suckle one nipple, then move to the other to repeat the action. She mewled with pleasure, jolting and shivering as he thumbed and sucked the tender peaks.

"Take off your clothes," she panted when he took a moment to pull away and catch his breath. "Now."

He laughed. "Ordering me around, are you?"

Her eyes narrowed. "Please, *please* take off your clothes."

He swallowed at the need in her voice, more intense than it ever had been before. He shoved off the bed and stripped out of his clothing in record time. When he rejoined her on the bed, she reached for his cock with a shudder of need. He let her stroke him a few times before he changed position.

He pulled her to a sitting position and kissed her as he maneuvered her. She opened her legs without resistance, lifting herself on his lap at his urging until his cock was at her entrance. More importantly, she was face-to-face with him in the most intimate of positions. They looked into each other's eyes as he slid deeply within her, encountering no resistance after all her excitement.

Her grip on his shoulders tightened and she moved to bury her face in the crook of his neck, but he lifted a finger to press beneath her chin.

"Look at me, Vivien," he whispered, his tone caught between an order and a plea.

For a moment, her stare was pure terror, but then she nodded. They locked gazes as he began to move. With the first stroke, pleasure tore through him, ricocheting through his body with an intensity that took him off guard. She responded to the thrust, riding him, milking him, letting him feel her pleasure and see the rising tide of it in her clear blue eyes. He felt entirely joined with her, more powerfully than he had ever felt before. It was intense, passionate, and above all else, loving.

He felt the flutters of her orgasm just as the hot burst of his own rose out of his control. Together they cried out, clinging to each other, lost in the other's stare, as their bodies jerked out of control. She pulled his seed from him with her wild thrusts and the only time she broke her gaze was when she tilted her head back and let out a low, hungry cry of pleasure that seemed to fill the room, fill his ears, fill his soul with satisfaction.

She fell forward against him, clinging to him as she buried her face in his bare shoulder. He leaned back, pulling her against him as he lay down. He expected her to move, to draw back, to excuse herself. Instead, she settled in against him and held him.

An hour had passed since they made love and Vivien remained against Benedict's side. She felt warm, safe, comfortable and for the first time in all her life, she did not want to run from those intense feelings. She sat up a fraction.

In the dying firelight, Benedict's face was relaxed in sleep. He was so handsome, so perfect.

She brushed a lock of hair from his forehead and he did not stir with the motion. She smiled, but the expression faded as a strong desire welled up in her. A desire to do something she had never done before.

She touched him again, to be certain he was not awake. When he didn't move or react, she leaned closer, her hands shaking.

"I love you," she whispered.

The words sounded so foreign coming from her mouth, from her voice. True, but foreign. And yet somehow comforting to finally admit out loud what she had felt for weeks. For years.

Suddenly exhausted, she cuddled against his side and let herself drift into sleep. Tomorrow might bring a whole new set of pains, but tonight she was happy. And tonight was enough.

CHAPTER 16

Vivien sat across from Benedict, staring as he ate his breakfast. She had never spent a night with him before. Never shared breakfast at his table. A fact he seemed to find as amazing as she did troubling.

He smiled. "You should eat some of that. Starving yourself won't change what you have done."

She shook her head. "What did I do?"

He raised an eyebrow. "I know you well enough to recognize that you are panicking over staying with me last night. It isn't your nature to share breakfast with someone."

"It is a delightful breakfast, though," she attempted weakly.

He seemed to see through her uncomfortable façade and smiled, though he didn't press her, which put her at ease enough to talk to him about the exact subject he had brought up.

"I don't know why I stayed," she said softly. "I wanted to be here. I wanted to be with you."

He lifted his head from his breakfast and stared at her for a long moment before he spoke. "I am glad of that."

"I need you, I suppose, more than I wish I did," she continued, the words catching in her throat even as she forced them out.

"I would give you anything you needed," he vowed.

"I know that to be true." She shook her head. "To your detriment. That's why I left in the first place. That's why we could never be together now."

He opened his mouth to argue that point, but her lifted hand stopped him.

"This is a subject we never agree upon. Why don't we avoid destroying this lovely moment?" When he nodded in acquiescence, she continued, "The fact is that there is something I must do and it may require your help."

He lifted his brows. "*You* require *my* help?"

She nodded, even though sound had begun to echo in her ears, including the wild pounding of her heart. "You must recognize how difficult those words are for me to say."

"I do," he said, his voice still filled with astonishment. "Which makes me believe this thing you will ask of me is very important, indeed. Please tell me what it is."

She swallowed. Had speaking always been this laborious? She could scarcely remember, her mind was so addled by what she was about to say.

"When we went on our picnic to the park in the outskirts of London, do you remember that I mentioned the village I grew up in was a short distance away?"

He nodded. "I do, for I was shocked you would share such a detail with me. You have always been protective of your past."

She blinked because she felt like the room was spinning. "I have been and I have reasons for that, I assure you. But being in that place, thinking about my home, has made me want to…go back."

Actually, that was not true. The last thing she wanted to do was return to that village. But her list included the item "revisit the past". Until she saw the place where she had grown up, where she had lost everything, where she had experienced the deepest despair of her life, she could not leave London. She could not start over. She had to put the past away, for good.

"You want to see your family?" he asked, brow wrinkling, for she knew he didn't understand.

She shook her head. "They are gone from there, moved years ago. No, I just want to go back to that place. But it is not going to be a pleasant visit, I fear. And I would like to have a—a friend with me."

"You consider me your friend," he said, his tone blank so she couldn't ascertain what his feelings on that statement were.

She nodded. "Perhaps the one who knows me best," she whispered and that was the truth.

Even Mariah and Lysandra didn't have the connection with her that she had somehow allowed with Benedict. It was a weakness, yes, but one her talk with Walter had helped her understand she had to accept, even if it was only for a little while.

Benedict got to his feet and moved toward her. She tensed as she awaited his response and was surprised when he dropped to his knees before her. He reached up and cupped her cheek.

"Vivien, I will go with you anywhere you ask."

Relief flooded her as she leaned her cheek into the roughness of his palm. All her nervousness fled at that simple touch, replaced by a peacefulness she had never known.

It was a somewhat terrifying prospect that he could draw such complicated and deep feelings from her. Her natural urge to distance herself kicked in and began to overwhelm her earlier surrender to her desire to be near him.

She pulled back. "There will be rules, though, if you go with me."

He met her stare for a moment and then laughed as though he had expected her retreat as much as he had not expected her surrender.

"Of course there are," he teased as he pushed to his feet and waved a hand for her to continue. "Please tell me what they are."

"You must not tell anyone we meet who I am or that I lived there as a girl," she said.

"Will they not recognize you?" he asked in confusion. "You only left ten years ago."

She shook her head. "I doubt they will. I wasn't close to anyone there and I have changed a great deal in my time away from Sapsgate."

A frown drew her lips down. There was no greater truth than the statement she had just made. She was not the same person at all.

"And what about—?" he began.

She shook her head. "My second request is that you ask me no questions," she interrupted with as much kindness as she could muster.

He lifted his brows. "So you wish me to come with you but say nothing to anyone we meet and ask you no questions," he repeated.

She nodded, though when she saw it in those terms, she could understand how cold her request was.

"Yes," she managed to squeak a bit sheepishly.

"Would you like me to be gagged during our visit?" he asked. "Just to be certain I wouldn't break these rules?"

She pushed from her chair and moved over to the place he had taken by the fire.

"Oh please don't be angry, I am not trying to offend. I..." She trailed off as she tried to think of a way to explain her confused and troubled heart to him. "This is not easy for me. But if my rules make it impossible for you to go with me, I do understand and I shall make the trip alone."

He took her hand and drew her closer. "I want to go with you, even if you will not allow me to actually be of some help to you. When do you wish to go?"

She hesitated. "I would have liked to do it today, but I realize it is past noon now and our start would be too late."

He nodded, but she could see he continued to be troubled. "I agree. The drive is a few hours and if you want any time to actually look around, do whatever it is you wish to do, you won't want to be there so late. But if you desire an immediate visit, what about tomorrow?"

Relief flooded her. Tomorrow she would cross this awful duty from her list.

"Yes, tomorrow."

"I will make the arrangements," he promised. "But I do have one question."

She drew in a sharp breath. "But I thought you understood that—"

"Yes, yes," he interrupted. "Your precious privacy on this subject. If you choose not to answer, that will be your prerogative. But I must know, why do you wish to do this immediately? You left that place ten years ago and only thought of it again recently. Why must you return so suddenly?"

She bit her lip, worrying the tender flesh. She couldn't explain herself to him. She couldn't say that she had to do everything on her list because before the end of the summer she would be gone, never to return. If she dared to reveal something so powerful, he would refuse to help her. He would do everything in his power to convince her to stay.

And she couldn't stay. For his sake as much as her own. It was clear to her now, after the past few intimate days, that he would never move on with his life if she was always there, reminding him that he loved her.

"Benedict, please accept that I simply must do this now. I have no other reason than I wish to do so."

She held her breath as she watched his face fall in disappointment and frustration. He wanted so much more than she could hope to give.

"Very well," he finally said softly. "Then you have the rest of your day free."

He moved to turn away, but she grasped his hand and held fast. "No, I don't," she whispered. "You see, if you would be able, I would like to spend the day with you."

He smiled down at her in surprise. "Would you? And what should we do?"

She could think of a dozen ways to entertain themselves in his bed, but instead she said, "I would like to continue enjoying London. With you."

He stared down at her, face unreadable, for so long that she feared she might have finally pushed him too far. That she had finally cut him off to the point where he no longer wished to pursue anything deeper with her than the passion that sparked between them.

But then he smiled. And she knew that he was hers, at least for a while longer.

Vauxhall Gardens burst with excitement and the chatter of the Great Waterfall bubbled behind the conversation of other visitors. Benedict smiled as Vivien clutched his elbow, looking around at the beautiful plants and buildings.

For the moment, it felt as though they were nothing but another courting couple, strolling through the gardens, enjoying the dusky end to a perfect day.

"These past few hours have been wonderful," Vivien breathed, mirroring his own thoughts perfectly. "I believe if I could never see London again, I would be content that I had experienced its best."

He laughed. "Why would you never be able to see London again?"

She shrugged one shoulder. "I don't know. Things happen and change, one can never know what will be around the next bend."

He took a sidelong glance at her. She was so difficult to read. They had been close all day, she had been relaxed and open in ways he had never expected. All it served to do was make him fall even more deeply in love with her, for he could see a future with her.

And yet she still held so much back. Everything that mattered.

"I suppose you are correct that we never know what is about to happen," he mused, treading carefully as he motioned to a bench where they would have the best view of the fireworks which were to start in a few moments. "Is that the reason why you have made so many decisions lately?"

She did not look at him and slowly slid her hand from the crook of his arm. "I do not think I have made so very many decisions of late."

He wrinkled his brow. Was she being truthful in that assessment, or merely hiding from him once more?

"There is your sudden desire to learn the city you have lived in a third of your life," he pointed out gently.

She shrugged. "Once I began seeking out the pleasures of London, it became a habit."

"And it has been mentioned more than once that the number of fetes at your home has been greatly reduced this Season," he pressed.

She laughed, though the sound was hollow. "I'm certain I am not missed, but my free entertainments and libations are."

He looked at her closely. She teased, but he could see that she truly believed no one who entered her home had any real feelings for her. A fact with which he did not fully agree. Several people had expressed genuine concern to him about Vivien's distraction.

"And then there is me," he continued, his voice soft.

The first explosion of fireworks burst overhead and Vivien jerked her face upward to look at the falling sparkles of colored fire. In the light of the rocket, he could see her drawn-down, sad face and it cut him to the bone.

"You returned to me after three years apart," he said, taking her hand from her lap and stroking his fingers over the top. "And you have allowed me to be closer to you than ever before. I do not complain about this, but I continue to wonder at your motives. Why now?"

This time, she faced him. Another firework exploded overhead, casting her face in a strange blue glow that did nothing to diminish the seriousness of her expression.

"Benedict, why ask these questions? Why can't you just be happy with the time we have left?"

He frowned at her odd turn of phrase. There was something quite final and dire about it. "The time we have left?" he repeated.

Even in the dim light, she blanched. "Today, this night," she said as a means of explanation.

One he did not believe. The more he pondered it, the more he realized there truly was some higher reason for her sudden shifts in attitude. And even though it was clear she had no intention of sharing those reasons with him willingly, he planned to find out on his own.

But not at this moment.

"Have you heard about Dershingham?" he asked.

She seemed surprise that he would change the subject, but also very relieved. "I've heard murmurings, why? Has something changed?"

He allowed himself a grin. "Somehow the truth about his financial situation was made public. In White's. By a creditor."

Her eyes widened. "Good Lord, I do need to have more parties if I am so far removed from such gossip. When did this happen?"

"Two nights ago. The man all but stormed in and demanded payments. Dershingham was at the card tables and had already lost three of his best horses and a secondary estate. He rose up and threatened the man and both of them were tossed out on their asses."

Vivien covered her mouth to hide a wide smile. "Great ruination."

"Indeed. If my sources are correct, his world is already crashing down around him. Loudly and with some level of finality. And it is all thanks to you, my dear."

"Thanks to us both," she said with a dismissive wave of her hand.

"Either way, it is a moment a long time coming."

She leaned closer and her eyes were lit up with more than triumph now. He recognized her desire for him sparkling there in the moonlight. "Do you know how I would like to celebrate and enjoy this moment?"

He shook his head, mesmerized and seduced by the feel of her breath on his neck.

"I can scarcely believe it to be true, but you and I have never made love in public before," she whispered against his ear. "I have heard there is a dark and private corner behind the concert hall where I would dearly love to feel you inside me while the fireworks explode above us."

She stood and offered her hand. A hand he took and did not resist against when she tugged him the short distance to the concert hall down the lane. Visitors sprawled on the steps, watching the fireworks with oohs and ahhs. Vivien ignored them and drew him around the back of the building.

The moment they were sheltered from the eyes of the others, she pushed him against the flat stone wall of the hall and lifted up on her tiptoes to kiss him with a passion that was unfiltered and wild. She was grasping for some of the control she had handed over to him with her emotions, but he wasn't about to allow her to take it back. Not now.

He spun her around until it was her back against the cool stone of the building. The crowd nearby ohhhed with delight at the explosion of a firework, and as Benedict cupped her backside and ground against her through their clothing, Vivien echoed that sound of pleasure.

His control faltered at the response and he struggled as he hiked at her skirts. She seemed to be just as affected, for she jerked at his trouser fly, maneuvering until his cock slipped free of the confines and she could stroke him.

He looked down as another firework bathed them in a strange green light. Her dress was up around her rib cage, his cock was naked and hard. He grinned as he lifted her and stroked, sliding into her body in one smooth motion.

She cried out, but the sound was lost in the noise of the crowd still appreciating the show just around the corner from them. The idea that any of them could come around the building and be scandalized to find the son of one of the most important families in London making love to his mistress excited him more than it should have.

He drove hard into her, setting a frantic rhythm, but she met him at every stroke, wrapping her arms around his neck and straining to keep up. She gasped with pleasure, she squeezed him as he entered and exited her willing body. And when she came, her face so close to his, he felt the reverberations of her pleasure through every part of him.

He held her close as she jolted and shivered, squeezing him through the crisis, crying out his name until he could no longer control his response. He exploded deep within her, their pleasure merging and becoming one as their bodies had.

Afterward, he held her, their foreheads pressed together and their breath slowing into one shared inhalation and exhalation. She drew back when a moment had passed. Fireworks exploded overhead and he saw all the joy in her features in the blue light.

"I am still swept away by you," she said with a tiny smile.

He hadn't expected that admission and he was taken aback by how honest it was. "I hope you always shall be."

Her smile faded and she leaned forward to bury her face in his shoulder. He held her close and vowed that he *would* determine what was driving her to make her more recent decisions. And when he did, he intended to do everything in his power to keep her close this time. To keep her in his life forever.

CHAPTER 17

Vivien stared at Benedict from the corner of her eye as the carriage they traveled in bumped over the roads. One phrase kept playing in her head over and over, disrupting everything and anything she believed about herself.

Two Nights. Two Nights. Two Nights.

She shook her head, but it continued to repeat itself, reminding her that she had spent not one but *two* nights in this man's company, that she had allowed herself to settle into his life as she had never done with anyone before.

The fact should have terrified her, but instead she was left with a strangely comforting feeling instead. Almost as if she belonged with him.

Even though she knew for a fact that could never be.

What *was* terrifying, though, was that they were less than fifteen minutes from their destination, the village of Sapsgate. During the last half-hour, they had left the main road and bumped along, inching toward her past. Inching toward painful memories she had long ago put away with never a thought that she would revisit them.

And yet she was now compelled to do so.

As if he sensed her discomfort, Benedict reached out to take her hand, slipping his fingers between hers before he rested their joined hands against his thigh. Immediately she was soothed and her nervousness faded, at least a little.

"So what kind of girl were you, Vivien?" he asked, his tone light as if to combat her somber mood.

She smiled. This question defied her rule that he not insert himself except when welcomed, but she appreciated his attempts to comfort her nonetheless.

"Probably very different than you picture me to have been."

He tilted his head. "Oh? I wonder at that. You see, I have always pictured you as a studious sort, perhaps even a tiny bit of a blue-stocking, for you are far too intelligent not to have studied and enjoyed the process of learning. I would wager, though, that you always dreamed of more, especially coming from such a tiny hamlet. Perhaps you even snuck peeks at the latest fashions and stole the Society paper when your mama wasn't looking."

Vivien's eyes widened and he chuckled. "How far off the mark am I?"

She could scarcely speak for a moment, but then stammered, "A-almost exactly right, actually. Though my mama encouraged me to read the Society papers, so I never had to steal them. But how did you guess?"

He wrinkled his brow. "What would you have thought I would say?"

"Most men would believe I lived a sinful life from my day of birth, considering how I turned out," she admitted with a shrug that did not betray how painful an assumption that had been.

He shook his head. "Most men have never attempted to look past your exterior show. And to their detriment, for to know you, even as little as you allow me, is a gift. You are intelligent, focused and as strong as any man I've ever known. Those things did not happen from some magical wave of a wand. They must have been built from a foundation of some kind."

She stared at him, surprised that her eyes filled briefly with tears. He loved her, *truly* loved her. With the kind of depth of feeling she had scoffed at in books or pretended only existed for others as she watched her best friends find love and true happiness with their husbands.

It made the fact they could not truly be together all the more unfair.

The carriage slowed and she breathed a sigh of relief. With his words and her recognition of his heart, the vehicle had become far too close and confining. She welcomed the opening of the door and the fresh air from outside as she stepped out and looked around.

The driver had stopped at a small inn that was central to Sapsgate, The Prided Pony. To her surprise, the place looked smaller than she remembered, but otherwise much the same. Even the paint on the sign was chipped in exactly the same way.

Benedict took her arm and looked up at the building and the street on which it stood with interest. "Not a bad center of town," he commented.

She followed his gaze. The other shops lined the main boulevard with a tailor, a general merchant and a doctor's office. All exactly as she recalled.

"How can a place be so stuck in time?" she murmured, more to herself than to him.

He shrugged regardless. "Ten years is a lifetime and also the blink of an eye. I would wager in twenty it will look differently and even more so in a hundred."

She would have nodded except at that moment the carriage began to pull away.

"Where is he going?" she asked, panic in her tone that she wished she could erase the moment she spoke it.

Benedict squeezed her arm gently. "Only to park the vehicle behind the inn and inquire about food and water for the horse. My man is to be at the ready, whenever you wish to depart. We are not abandoned here, I assure you."

She nodded and fought for a moment to control her emotions.

This place was not a safe one for her—she could ill afford to be wild with her heart.

"Of course," she said and was pleased that the tension was gone from her voice. "I expect this will not take long, but the animal must rest, of course."

He offered her an arm and she took it. "Where to first?" he asked.

She looked around. "I suppose the general merchandise store would be as good a place to begin as any."

He nodded as he led her there. He spoke about something benign, but she hardly heard his words as they neared the entrance. There was unpleasant history to this place.

They moved up the stairs and Benedict released her to open the door. She passed by him and into the goods store almost as if she were moving through a tunnel. A bell rang above her, the same one that had hung there when she lived in this place. The shop smelled the same too, like sweet candy and cheap fabric and tobacco smoke mixed together for a disparate, pungent scent.

She looked around. Goods lined the shelves.

"Welcome," a voice behind the counter said.

Vivien jumped and turned toward the person. It was Mrs. Carlisle, the same woman who had sat behind that counter a decade before. She was older now, but with the same questioning expression. Vivien held her breath as she waited to be recognized, but the woman didn't seem to see her as familiar.

"May I help you?" she pressed.

Vivien shook her head. "N-No," she stammered. "Just looking around."

Mrs. Carlisle hesitated, almost as if she was starting to remember something, but then shrugged. "Let me know if you need any help."

Vivien jerked out a nod and looked around a moment more. Finally, she turned to Benedict and said, "I think that's all."

He wrinkled his brow, but didn't argue as they left the store.

Outside, she glanced down the street. More memories cascaded down upon her, making her head spin as she pondered them all.

"The woman didn't know you," Benedict said softly.

Vivien shook her head. "I suppose I wasn't memorable," she said as a means to explain.

He didn't look convinced, but before he could respond, the door to the shop opened and a woman came running out. Vivien stared. The woman was Genevieve Carlisle. And from her expression, Vivien could see she remembered what her mother had not.

"As I live and breathe, I knew it was you when I heard your voice from the back," the woman said, her face lighting up. She rushed to Vivien and tugged her close in a tight hug "I heard you speak and I knew in an instant that you were Alice Roth."

Vivien's face was frozen in horror and heartbreak, but she hugged the woman back lightly, proving she knew the stranger. Her wide eyes darted to Benedict, judging what he had heard, what he thought of it all. He could do nothing but stare back.

Alice Roth? *Why* would this woman call her that? And why wasn't Vivien correcting her mistake?

Unless that was truly her name.

"It has been an age," the other woman said as she stepped away from Vivien and looked her up and down with clear appraisal. "So much has changed. Look at you! You are dressed all like a lady."

Vivien flushed darker than Benedict had ever seen and she shot another glance his way. He saw how naked she felt, how revealed by this woman's careless words, and he wished he could help her, but he was still spinning.

The woman turned to him and snapped her mouth shut. "Oh, I beg your pardon, I didn't even see you standing there. Is this your husband, Alice?"

Vivien opened her mouth, but Benedict could see that she was in no shape to answer such questions. He stepped forward and gently placed a hand on her back to comfort her.

"I am," he declared with more ease than he should have displayed in claiming her as a wife. "Benedict Greystone, at your service, Miss…?"

He held out his opposite hand and the woman shook it. "I'm Genevieve Winston, though Alice knew me as Carlisle. I married Martin Winston, can you believe it?"

Vivien shook her head. "I cannot," she whispered.

Others might have noticed her flat tone, her shattered expression, but Mrs. Winston did not. She continued to chatter on, unfettered.

"You must be here to see your mother."

Vivien blanched even further. "My—my mother? But she moved away!"

Now Mrs. Winston did hesitate at the strength of Vivien's statement.

"You did not know she returned?" Mrs. Winston's face was filled with triumph that she had obtained some kind of gossip. "She did, a few months ago. She's back in your old home. Come, we must go see her. I'll tell Mama and be right back to walk with you."

With a quick smile, the woman hurried back into the shop, leaving Vivien and Benedict alone. She turned toward him, looking up into his face.

He was shocked by what he saw. She was pale, eyes rimmed red by tears she was holding back, she looked terrified, sick and utterly lost.

"Please do not ask me questions," she whispered. "Not now. Not yet."

He brushed her cheek with the back of her hand. "I want to help you, Vivien. That is my only wish."

She nodded, but they could speak no more as Mrs. Winston returned to their side with a laugh. "Mama was amazed that it was you, Alice. She thought you seemed familiar but with your fancy hair and clothes, it's like you're another person entirely."

"Yes," Vivien said, her tone flat. "I often feel like another person."

"Come, I'll walk with you. You must be thrilled to see your mother."

Vivien took Benedict's arm and they walked along the road with Mrs. Winston chattering on about people whose names Vivien had never spoken to him but had obviously been important during her youth. Vivien never responded except to nod or shake her head, but her silence did not stop Mrs. Winston from prattling on endlessly.

Finally, after about a mile of walking, they reached a small, tidy home on the edge of the village. At the gate, Vivien stopped and stared. Benedict saw the pain she had exhibited in the village double.

"I know your mama is home," Mrs. Winston buzzed. "Let us ring the bell."

Vivien didn't move and Benedict stepped forward. "You have been so kind to walk with us, Mrs. Winston, but Viv—Alice has not seen her mother in some time. Perhaps you would allow us a bit of privacy in her reunion?"

Vivien snapped her gaze to him and he saw her relief. Mrs. Winston seemed perturbed, the way a gossip always did when she was cut off from a source of news. And Benedict had no doubt that was just what she was, harmless but thrilled to have seen Vivien first so she could share all her observations with her sewing circle.

"Of course," she said, for there was no other proper answer. "But I hope you will come see me during your stay. I assume you *will* be staying?"

Vivien shook away whatever she was thinking. "No!" she burst out.

Mrs. Winston took a step back at the strength of her response and Benedict hurried to fill the gap Vivien had created.

"Unfortunately, my business does not allow us to escape London for more than a day. But I'm certain we will see you again. It has been such a pleasure."

Even this woman could not misunderstand his dismissal. She appeared perturbed as she stepped back.

"Very well. It was nice to see you, Alice. I hope you will say goodbye before you depart."

Vivien nodded blankly. "Of course."

The other woman started back up the road toward the main center of the village and Benedict breathed a sigh of relief.

"I cannot imagine you being friends with that woman, even when you were a girl," he muttered. "I do not picture you as that foolish."

Vivien swallowed. "I was foolish enough, in my own way. But I would not have counted Genevieve as a bosom friend, no. She always talked far too much."

They stared at the house together.

"We can leave," he said softly. "I could have the driver ready in a moment and we could be home to London before sunset."

He could see her pondering the value of his suggestion, and how much she longed to run from whatever awaited her in this house, but instead she shook her head.

"I came here to face my past," she murmured, more to herself than to him. "I must do that to move on."

He wrinkled his brow at her choice of words. Move on? Where was she moving on to?

But he held his tongue, keeping his questions to himself because at present he didn't think she could bear them. Instead, he touched her hand as they walked up to the front door of the little cottage.

"I am here," he whispered.

She looked up at him. "It is the only fact that makes this tolerable," she admitted with a weak smile.

Then she lifted her hand and knocked on the door.

CHAPTER 18

Vivien could barely breathe as the door opened and revealed a servant she did not know. But of course, when her mother moved away, she likely had left what few servants she had behind, only to hire new ones upon her return.

"May I help you?" the maid who stood at the entryway asked blandly, completely oblivious to Vivien's pain and horror in this moment.

"I—I am here to see…to see my mother," she stammered.

She shot a brief glance over her shoulder to find Benedict watching her with the same unreadable expression as he had possessed all day, despite the revelations he had heard. She bit her lip and forced herself to continue.

"I'm Alice Roth," she finished, hating the way her given name rolled from her tongue.

Benedict drew a sharp intake of breath at her admission, but said nothing else.

The maid stared at her with wide eyes, then bobbed out a brief nod. "I will ascertain if Mrs. Roth is home."

She left the door open but didn't ask them in and so Vivien

stood on the step, silent as she waited for the girl's return. It was but a moment, though it felt like an eternity, when she was back.

"Come with me," she said, her tone darker than it had been as she gave Vivien a quick once-over before she led them both into the house.

Vivien felt her entire body tense as she moved into the foyer. The house looked the same, it smelled the same, and she felt like she had stepped back in time to a far more unpleasant period.

The parlor was on the right and as the door opened, Vivien briefly considered running. Benedict would aid in her escape, she knew that. Except she feared she had gone too far now. If she left, she wouldn't leave the past behind as she had before. She had opened this Pandora's Box, she had to face the demons within.

They entered the parlor and Vivien moved to the window to stare out at the gardens behind the house. So many memories mobbed her that she hardly noticed anything else in the room until Benedict cleared his throat.

"You do not have to stay," he said to the maid.

Vivien turned to find that the girl had positioned herself next to the open door, arms folded, as she stared at the two of them.

The maid pursed her lips. "I have orders, sir."

Benedict looked utterly confused, but Vivien squeezed her eyes shut as frustration and anger overtook her. She moved forward.

"Thinks we'll steal her silver, does she?" she snapped.

The maid took a faltering step back at Vivien's tone, but did not respond.

Vivien pivoted back to the window. "Ridiculous."

"Not so very ridiculous when you consider all you've done," her mother's voice said from the door. Vivien swallowed hard and turned to look at her.

Rosalind Roth was much the same as she had been the last time Vivien stood in this parlor. Tall and slender with blonde hair like her own, but rather than blue eyes, she had dark brown ones. Time had been kind to her, keeping her face freer from lines than some women of her advancing years.

Her expression was also the same—filled with hate and judgment for the daughter she despised.

"Mother," she managed to say with at least some strength to her tone. "You look well."

Her mother sniffed in reply and motioned the maid away. "Thank you, Ruth, you may go. Don't worry yourself with tea—I doubt our *guests* will stay long."

Vivien lifted her chin to keep her pain from being reflected on her face, but her embarrassment was harder to control. Especially when Benedict's horror and shock at this exchange was more than evident on his handsome face. But of course it would be, he came from a loving family, he couldn't fathom the deep flaws present in hers.

"You are correct, we will not trespass on your hospitality long," Vivien spat out, nearly choking on the words. "I was nearby and did not realize you continued to make your home here. I would not have bothered you had I been forewarned."

Her mother's eyes narrowed. "Indeed, I suppose you did not know I was here. The last you heard was that I left Sapsgate. Did it give you pleasure to know that what you did drove me away from the home your father built for us?"

Benedict stepped forward at that. "Mrs. Roth, perhaps you do not understand—" he began.

Vivien gasped as her mother turned her attention on him. She hadn't seemed to notice him before that moment, a fact that Vivien had wished would remain the same. Now her mother looked him up and down.

"What are you?" she asked, the cold steel of her tone unbendable, even by his charm. "Her lover? Not her husband, I'm certain."

If Benedict was shocked by her directness, he did not show it on his face. "I am her…" He glanced at Vivien with a supportive smile. "I am her friend."

"Her friend," her mother sneered. "Is that what they call a whore's consort now?"

Benedict drew back in horror, his face twisting with shock at her mother's pointed, cruel words.

"Stop," Vivien said softly. "Your quarrel is with me, not him."

"Protective indeed," her mother all but hissed. "But does he know you are a murderer?"

Vivien rubbed her eyes with one hand. "I did not murder anyone."

"You did," her mother protested in something akin to a screech. She spun back on Benedict. "You know that she spread her legs for the first man who offered her a little more than a smile, don't you? And that it destroyed any hope her father had for marrying her well to a very nice young man of good fortune. Instead, my husband had an apoplexy and died in our dining room because of the public reaction to the fact she had been compromised."

Vivien swallowed. Her mother's revisionist version of that night made her throat dry and her eyes sting with tears she refused to shed because she knew they would give her mother such pleasure to see them.

"I had to leave Sapsgate because I couldn't bear living in the house where my love took his last breath," her mother continued, her anger growing with every word. "Where our own child stood over him with such lack of feeling and let him die because she had no principles."

Vivien clenched her fists. "I felt his death as keenly as anyone," she protested, her voice cracking. "I wept for him."

Her mother shook her head. "Little good that did, to weep for him in death when you were the one to put him in the grave." She spun on Benedict. "So remember that, my fine gentleman. If you think she has any kind of a heart, she does not. She is an empty, worthless shell. You would do well to watch your back that she doesn't stab it just for the pleasure of causing you pain."

"Enough!" Benedict roared in a tone Vivien had never heard before.

She spun on him to find his face almost purple with rage and his bright eyes flashing. She stepped back, stunned by the power of his emotions, the drive he had to protect her. And even her mother, with all her limitations, recognized it and staggered away a step.

"You will not say another word," he continued. "Viv—" He stopped and cast a quick glance at her. "Your daughter is no empty shell. She is as full and glorious a woman as I have ever met. She is kind and decent, she helps those who need her and she would never cause harm to anyone unless it was in the defense of the weak. I refuse to let you attack her with such vitriol, no matter who you are."

Her mother wobbled briefly, but then shook her head. "You don't know her."

He looked at Vivien and she could see that he believed her mother on some level. In fact, she was right in so many ways. But in others, in important ways, she was wrong.

He shook his head. "With all due respect, neither do you. You may be correct that I don't know the circumstances of her past, but neither do I care about them. I know her today."

Her mother opened and shut her mouth, but couldn't seem to come up with a response to Benedict's declaration. Slowly, Vivien approached her.

"Mother," she whispered, wanting so much to take her hand but unable to breach the gap that would always be between them. "I should not have come today, for I know my presence troubles you and I do not wish to do that to you. I realize you have lost a great deal and that you blame me for that."

Her mother let out her breath in a shuddering sigh and did not lift her face to look at her daughter. Vivien hesitated a moment before she continued.

"Are you in need of funds?"

Her mother jerked her head up and Benedict shot her a glance too.

"No!" Her mother said, but then shifted slightly. "I would rather not receive money from the sources you obtain it from."

Vivien shook her head. "I will have a sum deposited into your account when I return to London. You can pretend you do not know the source."

Her mother folded her arms and said nothing. Not that Vivien expected appreciation, but the continued disgust from a woman who had once loved her stung.

"We'll go," she whispered as she moved for the door. She felt Benedict a step behind her and was glad he made no move to touch her. His warm hand on her back might have been her undoing. "I don't think I shall see you again, so I hope you will be well."

Her mother cast her one brief glance and then turned her face, cutting off contact, making it clear that the loss of her daughter was meaningless. Vivien nodded and exited the room.

The maid who had escorted them in was waiting for them in the hall. With a glare, she motioned for the door. Vivien might have laughed at the lack of subtlety if it all didn't hurt so damn much. That was something she had always wished to control, but had never been able to succeed at.

The air outside felt cool after the stifling environment of the parlor and Vivien drew a long breath of the freshness. Behind her, the front door to her childhood home slammed and she shut her eyes at the violence of the action, at the implications of it. She had revisited the past, just as her list had required she do, but in doing so she had rung the final bell on her relationship with her mother. She would never return here, she would never see her again.

And as she turned to Benedict to take the arm he offered and walked with him back toward the center of town and his carriage, she realized that she was going to have to tell him something about what he had witnessed, why everyone called her by a different name. She owed him that. And she did not look forward to the confessions she was about to make.

~

Benedict was thrumming with questions, but he said nothing until the carriage door closed and they began the long journey back to London. In the dim cool of the vehicle, he reached across to take Vivien's hand.

She looked up and her eyes were so sad that it hurt him to look into them.

"You want to know," she whispered. "You desire explanations for what you have seen and heard today."

He nodded. "It would be difficult not to desire them given all that has transpired," he admitted.

She swallowed and he saw her struggle on her face. Vivien had worked hard to control everything and anything she revealed to those in her life. Confession was not something she made easily and now the pain of it was palpable.

"You must realize by now that I was not always Vivien Manning," she began, her voice trembling.

"Yes," he said, squeezing her fingers.

"Alice Roth is the name I was born with and lived with for the first eighteen years of my life." She shook her head. "That girl, *Alice*, was a very different person than I am. She was raised by middle-class merchants with some success in their shop. They wanted her to marry a boy of status elevated from theirs, joining the riches of two families and providing them with a means to move up in local Society."

Benedict nodded. "You wanted something different."

She laughed. "Actually, I didn't. I had been raised to do as my parents requested. They were harsh taskmasters—I never believed there was another way but to obey and make up in some way for the disappointing fact that I was their only child and a girl on top of that."

He pursed his lips. "So what prevented your following their plan for you?"

"A man," she said, her breath short. She turned her face from him to stare outside at the passing green hills and trees. It was a lovely scene, but her voice contained no pleasure. "A boy, but I thought he was a man. He was the second son of a second son, of little importance to your Society but of great importance to mine. He was visiting family in the shire and we met in town. He pursued me and I convinced my parents that his star was on far faster a rise than the young man they wished me to marry."

He wrinkled his brow. "So you wished to raise yourself to loftier places. It is understandable."

"No," she laughed, utterly humorless. "I was not so wise as I am now. His loftier standing was nothing to me. I believed he cared for me. And when he cornered me in a barn at a country dance, I did not resist at first. We were in love, after all, or so I told myself. But when he went too far in his attentions, I refused him."

Benedict shut his eyes. "And he violated you regardless."

"Yes."

She stopped talking for a moment and he could see she was reliving whatever had happened to her that night so long ago. And despite all the pleasures she had given and received since that time, she was still moved by the memories. Memories he wished he could erase for her.

"Afterward, I put on my clothes and asked him when we would wed," she said. "I was terrified and in pain, but I believed he had a right if he was to be my husband. He laughed at me and it was clear he had never intended to be an honest suitor. He wanted my virginity and that was all. Once he took it, stole it, there was nothing left for him to desire."

She straightened her spine and he felt her attempt to put all her strength back into herself after her confession. But there was a new vulnerability there only he could see.

"But I still don't understand the estrangement between you and your family," he pressed. "Your mother was almost wild with her anger toward you."

"My mother…" She sighed. "She was always a little mad, overly emotional, painfully critical. She blamed me for the stress on our family if only for the fact that I was a girl. My father was a balance for her and we were often partners in an attempt to calm her."

"You told them what had happened?" he asked.

She nodded. "When I came home, my dress torn and my face streaked with tears, I had no choice but to answer their questions. My father was appalled, as was my mother. But in her mind, it was the loss of a future that was the true horror. We had turned aside my prior suitor because of the belief that this gentleman's son would wed me. Now I had no suitor and no virginity. I was ruined and so were they."

Benedict shuddered. "That could not have been her true thoughts. She felt no compassion for you in the attack?"

"Compassion is not an emotion she has ever truly felt. Perhaps she is not able," she said with a shrug that had to be more dismissive than those words made her feel. "But her cruelty only increased after that. She railed and shouted, she cried and called for friends to pity her. Of course that let the story be shared and verified and soon it was clear I could *never* marry well. My mother called me a whore and that is what I was in the eyes of everyone in Sapsgate."

"Great God," he muttered, stunned by her words. He might struggle with his family bonds, but his mother loved him. His brother loved him. He did not doubt those things for a moment.

She shrugged. "My father was sitting in the dining room a few weeks later, my mother screaming at me, railing on about how our lives were ruined. He suddenly stiffened and fell to the floor, dead before his napkin fluttered down beside him. The doctors called it an apoplexy, my mother said I murdered him. That night I slipped from the house with what few belongings I could carry and went to London on a post carriage. I have never returned."

"You changed your name," he said.

She nodded. "I changed everything. I became a new person. I all but killed poor Alice Roth, left her behind in Sapsgate. Vivien Manning was born and I have been her since the moment the carriage pulled down the road."

Benedict examined her face in the dim light from the window. Her voice was utterly calm, but he could see the strain around her eyes. She feared his reaction to all she had told. She feared the new intimacy that telling had created between them.

"I *like* Vivien Manning," he said softly as he reached out to caress her cheek.

She smiled slightly. "So do I," she admitted. "She is far stronger than I ever thought I could be."

"She certainly is strong as well as kindhearted." He shook his head. "Why did you offer your mother money after all her unkind words to you?"

She pondered that for a moment. "Because she is a sick woman, troubled by demons that existed long before my innocence was stolen in a barn. When my father was alive, she had someone to take care of her, to temper her worst impulses. Now she is alone and her torments must be her only companions. I pity her more than hate her. Though I cannot say that I did not loathe her for a very long time." He shook his head and she frowned. "You do not approve?"

He lifted his gaze to hers in surprise. "I approve of you enormously. And the fact that you have shared this very private view of yourself is something I appreciate. I realize it was not easy to do."

She had been sitting across from him in the carriage, but now she slipped over to his seat. Settling her head into the crook of his shoulder, she spread her fingers out across his chest and sighed.

"In truth, it was easier to share this with you than I ever thought it would be," she admitted. "I certainly did not expect I would end up confronted by my mother, with you standing by defending me, but since it has happened, I can truly say there is no one else I would have rather had at my side in that unguarded moment."

He leaned down to kiss the top of her head, breathing in the sweet scent of her hair. A swell of love washed over him, brought on by her trust and her strength.

"I would not have wished to be anywhere else," he whispered. "Now rest. I'll wake you when we reach London."

The events of the day had already taken their toll, for instead of arguing, Vivien settled closer, her breath heavy and slower as she drifted away into what he hoped would be a dreamless sleep. He settled into a more comfortable position and held her all the way to London.

Vivien handed her wrap over to Nettle and smiled at her butler. If he had an opinion about the fact that she had spent two nights away from home, when in the years he had served her she had barely spent one away, he said nothing about it.

"I trust nothing was amiss during my absence?" she asked.

"No, miss," he reassured her. "Though you did have quite a few cards left for you."

With a sigh, she took the stack he held out on a silver tray. She would end up throwing away the lion's share of invitations and requests for her company anyway, but the chore of going through them all still fell to her.

"Thank you," she said with a smile for him that was not forced. "Would you bring tea to my personal parlor?"

"Indeed," he said with a quick bow. "I shall have it prepared immediately."

She began to flip through the cards as she moved up the stairs toward her private chambers. As she expected, most were invitations to gatherings, inquiries into when her next party would occur and even one rather blunt and bold solicitation of her company.

She sighed as she sat down in the comfortable settee beside her fire and sorted the piles into correspondence she would answer and what she would not even bother issuing a response to.

As she sorted the cards, the door to her chamber opened and her maid, Rachel, came in with a tray laden with tea and cakes. The girl set it down and took a quick glance at the open door before she edged toward her.

"What is it?" Vivien asked, surprised by her normally light-hearted maid's odd behavior.

"This message came for you yesterday," she whispered and held out another envelope.

Vivien pushed to her feet and took the message. She recognized the address of her solicitor scribbled across the front of the envelope. She glanced up and motioned for Rachel to shut the door.

The girl did so and only then did Vivien say, "My solicitor sends messages here regularly—why the secrecy?"

"The boy he sent over to deliver it must have been an assistant," Rachel explained. "He was talking about houses in Italy when he brought it to the door."

"Oh great God!" Vivien said, blanching as she gripped the paper until it crumpled in her fingers. "What did Nettle say?"

"Nettle wasn't the one who answered the door. He had gone to visit a friend while you were away from home," Rachel explained. "It was Mrs. Pratt who answered and I jumped in and took the missive for you myself before she could understand what the man meant."

Vivien squeezed her eyes shut. Mrs. Pratt was her housekeeper, and at least she was a discreet woman.

"I told the messenger that he should not share a lady's private information with her servant," Rachel continued. "And he was quite rude, but he did shut his running mouth and present me with the letter. I would have left it with the other correspondence on your tray, but I didn't want any of the other servants to somehow stumble upon it."

"I appreciate that," Vivien said and opened the letter. She unfolded the sheets of paper within and read the first out loud.

"Dear Miss Manning, After much search, we believe we have found a situation in Italy to meet your stated needs. Enclosed find the particulars and a few artist's drawings of the home. Yours, etc.'"

She looked up at Rachel before she turned to the second sheet. "You are the only other person who knows about my plans at present," she said, uncomfortable in this attempt at intimacy, even though she wanted to share the moment with someone. "Would you like to see the house?"

Rachel nodded. "I would!"

Vivien drew a long breath and turned to the second sheet, a line of descriptives and figures on cost, which she skipped until she came to the first drawing of the home. She caught her breath. The little house in Naples was perfection. Beautifully built and with gardens along the front, it cried out as private and cozy, exactly what she had been seeking.

"But what about Napoleon?" Rachel asked as Vivien handed her the sketch. The maid cooed even though her question had not been answered.

Vivien waved her hand dismissively. "With enough money, anything can be done, even during a war."

She looked at the second sketch, a small collection of beautiful sites in the area near the house itself. She pictured herself walking the streets, buying bread, roaming the parks and museums of the city. Except in her mind she was not alone.

Benedict was with her.

She shook her head and shoved the paper toward Rachel before she got to her feet.

Rachel nodded over the images and then set the papers aside. "So this is the place then, isn't it?"

Vivien hesitated. The location was everything she had requested from her solicitor, and yet she felt less than satisfied.

"I...don't know..." she admitted, more to herself than to Rachel.

The maid moved closer. "Are you having second thoughts, miss?"

There was a hopefulness in her maid's voice that was unmistakable and Vivien turned to look at her with a smile. "I do not really know. The Season is only a few weeks old and already I have completed nearly every duty on the list we compiled together. Now this house has fallen into my lap and it makes the idea of leaving London so very real. Can I do it?"

Rachel tilted her head. "I cannot imagine you unable to do anything you put your mind to, miss. Though I admit, I would rather you stay. I realize if you left London to begin a new life, you would likely not take any of your current staff with you. And I do like working for you, miss."

Vivien touched the girl's hand briefly. "Thank you, Rachel. I appreciate that more than you know, for I realize that working for a woman such as myself must be trying at times."

Her mind trailed for a moment. A woman such as herself. Right now she didn't know who that woman was anymore. This final Season should have been about frivolity and fun, but instead all she could do was focus on Benedict, and allow herself feelings that could only bring her harm.

Even now, the idea of leaving him behind had her in a panic of sorts. It pressed on her chest and made her long to see him, touch him, remind herself that he was still hers, even for a short time.

She shook her head. "For now I shall set this aside and think on it before I respond to the solicitor."

There was relief on her maid's face as she handed the paperwork over to Vivien. "I shall keep my knowledge to myself as long as you'd like, Miss Vivien."

"I know that." Vivien smiled. "Now will you fetch Livermore? I have a message I need to write to someone and I'd like him to deliver it immediately."

Rachel hurried from the room to do her bidding and Vivien sat down at her escritoire to pen a missive. Not to her solicitor, but to Benedict. Because all these thoughts of leaving made her long to see him.

And that longing did not seem to be anything she could deny to herself. Not anymore.

~

Benedict stared up at the ceiling as he tried with all his might not to explode at his brother. He'd found Derek waiting for him when he returned from his outing with Vivien an hour ago. Ever since, his brother had been calmly talking to him.

Talking *at* him was a better descriptive. He'd been regaled with reminders on his place in life, on Vivien's place, on his promises to seek out a bride this Season…on everything and anything that was private in his life.

How he was able to rein in his frustration was truly a miracle. Finally, his brother paused to draw breath and Benedict looked at him.

"Is there a reason you hate Vivien so much, or is it just her place in life that makes you despise her?" he asked.

His brother hesitated and true surprise came to his eyes. "I—I do not hate Vivien," he stammered.

"Don't you?" Benedict asked, rising to pace the room. "Because I don't think you have ever expressed a positive word about her. You rail on and on about her and yet you do not know her at all."

Derek considered that a moment. "I know what she presents to the world."

Benedict looked at him over his shoulder. "If people always went by that, everyone would believe you to be a bore."

His brother chuckled. "Well, that may be true," he conceded. "But there is a difference between being seen as a bore and being seen as…"

He trailed off but the word hung in the air between them. The same word her mother had used to describe her. *Whore.* He flinched at the thought of it, especially now that he knew so much more about Vivien's history.

"She is not a whore, she is a survivor," he said softly.

Again his brother was quiet and Benedict could feel him treading lightly, trying to find the right way to say what he wished without starting a war, without closing Benedict's ears and mind.

"Perhaps you are right that I do not know her. That we are all far more than the faces we present to Society and the world at large. But I do know *you*, Benedict, you cannot deny that."

"As much as I sometimes want to, no I cannot. You are my brother and one of my best friends," Benedict acknowledged. "Which is why your opinion on this matter troubles me so much."

Derek nodded. "I realize you think that I am like Mother, that I only want to see you married properly and producing spares in the background just in case the unthinkable happens."

Benedict drew back a fraction at his brother's cold assessment of their mother's desires. "You do not truly think those are her thoughts."

Derek arched a brow. "Being the oldest, I hear far more of them. Does she care for me, for us? Of course. But she also cares about ensuring the continuation of Father's line. At this moment that means her top concern is marriage and children for all of us."

Benedict shuddered. "I suppose I hadn't thought of it in that manner. In truth, I have been avoiding spending more than a short time with her since she decided I should begin to search for a bride seriously this Season."

"You mean since you began spending all your time with Vivien Manning," his brother said softly. When Benedict said nothing in return, his brother continued, "The point is that her desires may be a bit...mercenary, but mine are not. I remember what you went through when your affair with this woman ended three years ago."

Benedict pursed his lips and returned to his place on the settee across from his brother. "And now that you've said this, let me remind you that I also know *you*. Although we are only two years apart in age, you have spent a lifetime trying to manage every aspect of my life. You have big brothered me until I sometimes wanted to scream, though I appreciate the sentiment behind all that protection and direction."

Derek smiled, but Benedict ignored that and continued.

"The problem is, dear brother, this time I do not need, nor do I ask for your counsel. You cannot control this, force this or manage this, no matter how much you might desire it. Who I am with and why I chose to be with her is really none of your business."

Before his brother could argue that fact, the door to the parlor opened and Benedict's butler stepped inside the parlor.

"Yes, Evans?" Benedict asked, though he kept his focused stare on his brother, who did the same right back at him.

"I am sorry to intrude, sir, but a message was just delivered."

Benedict kept his gaze on Derek. "I shall read it later, Evans. Place it on the sideboard on your way out."

"I will do so, sir, but the man who brought it said it was urgent. It is from Miss Vivien."

Benedict wrenched his stare from Derek and pushed to his feet. "From Vivien?" he repeated.

Evans held out the letter. Her handwriting was swirled and delicate across the paper and he soaked in the way she had written his name like it was a caress.

"Thank you. Is the man still here waiting a reply?" he asked as he tore the seal and slipped the note out.

"No, he has returned home." Evans bowed from the room and left Benedict to his letter...and his brother.

I realize my man's statement of urgency may have alarmed you, she began without a greeting of any kind. *I assure you I am well. But I do wish to see you immediately, if you can manage it. Yours, V.*

Benedict stared at the sign off. *Yours.* He had always wanted her to be his. And right now her call to him was more important than anything else.

He turned on his brother as he placed her letter into his pocket, holding it there for a moment.

"I'm sorry, Derek, but I'm afraid I must go."

His brother pushed to his feet and stared at him. "We are in the middle of a rather important conversation. You cannot leave in half an hour?"

"No," Benedict said simply, without further explanation. "You may finish your tea, of course, and have the run of my home. Evans and the others will fetch you anything you'd like—"

"I'm not talking about tea," his brother interrupted in frustration.

Benedict shrugged. "Good evening, Derek. Tell Jocelyn I passed along my highest regards."

He left his brother standing in the middle of the parlor, gaping after him as he called out his name. But as Benedict rushed outside and swung up on a waiting horse, he didn't care about the consequences his dramatic exit would cause.

All he cared about was responding to Vivien's siren's call.

When he arrived at her estate, Benedict was taken directly upstairs. He expected to be brought to her public bedroom or parlor, but instead Nettle motioned him to the private chamber he had seen a short time before. The very one he had asked to share with her, but she'd refused.

"Miss Vivien is waiting for you," the butler said, then bowed away and left him standing in the hallway, staring at the smooth surface of the door. He sucked in a deep breath and pushed inside.

Immediately, he staggered to a stop. Vivien stood in the middle of the room. She wasn't wearing a sensual nightshift or a deeply cut silken gown. She hadn't highlighted her already beautiful eyes with kohl or made herself look anything like the image she presented to the world. She stood before him in a plain, gray gown, her blonde hair done loosely so that strands of it fell around her shoulders. She smiled as he stepped inside the bedroom, but there was a nervousness to the expression.

"Are you well?" he asked as he stepped inside and shut the door behind him.

She nodded. "Yes." Her voice cracked. "I am fine. I hope I didn't worry you, I only…I wanted to see you."

"Here, in this chamber," he said, glancing around him.

She did the same. "I told you that someday I might allow this to be a place where we made love," she explained. "If you would still like to—"

He didn't allow her to finish. In three long steps, he crossed the room and drew her against him as he kissed her. He felt her surrender almost immediately and the sweetness of it nearly brought him to his knees.

Instead, he gathered her into his arms and carried her to the bed, *her* bed…the place where she truly slept and dreamed, and set her on the pretty brocaded coverlet with as much gentleness as he would use if she were his innocent bride.

He continued to kiss her, tasting her, letting the desire he felt inside him begin to boil before he stripped her of her gown or touched her intimately. His actions seemed to frustrate her as she squirmed to get closer, cupping the back of his head and encouraging him for a deeper, more passionate kiss.

Her fingers trailed up his stomach and she began to unbutton his shirt, their kisses continuing through her work, building to a crescendo of passion that drove him to want her, take her, make her his.

She stripped his shirt away with a throaty sound of satisfaction and only then did he pull away to stare down at her. Her eyes were bright with wanting, but she didn't look like the experienced mistress he had taken so many times. She looked fresh and young and so beautiful that it hurt him.

"Why are you looking at me that way?" she asked softly.

He smiled. "I was thinking how lucky I am to be here. With you."

Her own smile wavered slightly, but she never broke eye contact as she reached behind her and expertly unhooked the first two buttons on her gown. He followed suit and stripped the others free. Her dress drooped as she shrugged out of it and the chemise beneath. It was more than he could bear and he fell against her, pushing her back to recline on her pillows as his kisses rained down on her throat and to the curves of her breasts.

~

Vivien gasped as Benedict sucked one hard nipple between his lips. Her reaction wasn't only from the pleasure his action created, which was intense and powerful, but from the fact that his touch seemed so...*new*.

She almost sobbed as he pushed her dress lower and pressed his warm lips to her belly, her hip, baring her and lavishing attention on every inch of skin he revealed.

She was being worshipped and she reveled in it. Her legs fell open as he tugged her dress away and tossed it over the side of the bed. Heat filled her cheeks as he stared at her nude form. How long had it been since she felt awkward about her body? Years, almost a decade, and yet with him she felt shy.

It was a gift, and she repaid it by leaning closer and unfastening his trousers. As they fell away, she smiled, her sensual side reviving with need at the hard, heavy cock which greeted her. She had done this to him. Made him want. Made him hers.

And she intended to take full advantage.

She leaned back to the pillows and beckoned him toward her. She didn't have to ask twice. He covered her, driving his tongue between her lips at the same moment that he arched his hips and slid home in the wet heat of her body. Almost immediately, the shudders of an orgasm overtook her. She fought them, wanting to build pleasure with him, to anticipate it, but she couldn't fight the tide. With a cry, she arched against him, hips stroking wildly, fingernails digging into his flesh as she came with a power and intensity she could not recall experiencing before.

He smiled down at her as she moved through her crisis, stroking gently in order to prolong the release. Only when her final shuddering cry had echoed in the room did he began to thrust into her with any kind of earnest intent. The desire and pleasure that had just reached its crescendo began to build as he circled his hips in teasing movements. She met the thrusts, focused on the joining of their bodies, on him, on the fact that they were in her bed, in her room...

And without warning, the second release mobbed her. This time he didn't coax her through it. Instead, his thrusts increased, his breathing heavy against her neck, and with a harsh cry, he burst within her, their release merging as they continued to writhe together through the final shivering explosions of orgasm.

With a groan, he flopped on his back and pulled her with him. Vivien cuddled into the crook of Benedict's arm with a satisfied sigh. She had never made love to a man in her own bed before. It felt new and fresh, like the first time.

But his tension was palpable as he stroked fingers over her bare shoulder.

"I felt your desperation," he said softly.

She swallowed hard. He was not wrong about that emotion. Now that her list of items to do was almost finished, her promise to leave London loomed over her. She would never see him again if and when that time came.

But she wasn't going to tell him that. He would only muddy the already cloudy waters of her decision.

"It was desire you felt," she reassured him.

He shook his head and looked down at her. "I am no fool, Vivien. I know what it was. Please, you have trusted me with secrets, you have trusted me to take me to your own bed...couldn't you trust me with the truth about what is going on with you? Perhaps I could help."

She stared into his face. He wanted to support her. Perhaps he was the only man who had wanted it without an ulterior motive.

And she loved him for it. But if she confessed all, there would be only one end. He would tell her to stay. She probably would. And nothing would change. They could no more be together now than they ever could have.

At least, that was what she had always believed. Now her certainty felt cloudier.

"Sometimes it is best to leave things unsaid," she murmured, stroking the lines of his bare chest with the tip of her finger. She could touch it for hours.

She did not have the opportunity. He sat up and stared down at her, frustration as clear as his desire had been a few short moments before.

"Damn it, Vivien, you do vex me," he blurted out.

She stared as he climbed from her bed and began to dress himself with jerky movements.

"I do not understand you," he continued. "Why do you bother taking these steps forward when you only intend to retreat? I do not know what to think. Do you care for me or not? Do you want me or not? Do you trust me or not?"

She stared at him as she sat up and covered herself with the sheet. "Benedict," she began.

"You know I love you," he snapped and the world cut to half time.

He had said the words to her before, a very long time ago. Then they had caused a panic in her. Fear that reached her very core.

Today they brought something else. Something more dangerous. They brought her hope. Foolish and empty hope, for she knew, perhaps more than anyone, that love was not always enough. In fact, it rarely was.

"Benedict, you should not love me," she whispered. "You have a life to lead and it will have no room for me."

He shook his head. "Yes, so you have always told me. But you must have known that I still cared for you when you came to me that night at your party and asked me to come back to your bed.

Since I do not think you are a cruel woman, it makes me wonder… why? Why bring me back to your side? I think it is a question you should ask yourself since I am not allowed that privilege of inquiring about anything beyond the most surface subjects. And when you have an answer, please do contact me."

He grabbed his jacket from the back of the chair beside the door and strode from the room, leaving her staring at him, words left unsaid on her tongue. Words like, "I love you" and "Stay".

Words she couldn't say, not because she didn't feel them, but because they didn't belong to her. And she slipped to her side on the bed and wept with the pain brought both by his confession and by her realization that she could never be with him.

CHAPTER 20

Vivien stared at the ledger before her, adding up columns of numbers, making notations about additional payments her accountant should prepare and giving herself a general sense of her financial health. Most women of any station did not involve themselves in their household budget as she did, but she found that the absolute value of the numbers gave her some kind of peace. In math, there was a right and a wrong answer, no gray to muddy things.

And she needed that black-and-white view at present to calm her ever confused mind as it spun on questions of her future and her heart.

Her office door opened and Nettle stepped inside. "Miss Vivien, you have a visitor."

Vivien squeezed her eyes shut. She was in no mood to see anyone at present. She could barely stand to put on her public persona for an uninvited guest.

"Oh, please tell whoever it is that I am not in residence at present."

Her butler shifted slightly. "I would do so, madam, but it is Lord Abbotton who calls and he insists on waiting for you if you are not at home."

Vivien's hand hovered over the ledger until a drop of ink splashed down on the column she had been reviewing. With a curse, she jerked the quill aside and shook her head.

So, Derek had come. Of course he had.

"I see the problem," she said softly as she began to tidy up her work space. "Why don't you show the Earl to—"

She broke off. The public rooms in her home were designed to celebrate her position in Society, but with Derek she had always felt awkward and uncomfortable with herself. She didn't want him sitting in her parlor, staring at the erotic wallpaper and judging her even more harshly than he normally did.

"The terrace off the breakfast room is very pretty this time of year," Nettle provided with swift efficiency. "And the weather is warm and still, so he shall not be soaked or blown away during his time there."

Vivien nodded. "Yes, that should be perfect. Tell him I shall meet him there momentarily. And have tea brought. I doubt he'll lower himself to share in it, but we mustn't base our manners on the reaction of our guests, must we?"

Nettle nodded and his chin lifted with pride. "Indeed not. I shall bring a spread that will rival that which was served to the Queen today."

Vivien smiled as he executed a stiff bow and let himself from the room. Her servants had always been of the highest quality, with the kind of loyalty anyone would pray for. At least she didn't feel entirely alone as she put the ledger away and took a quick glance at herself in the mirror.

Since she was not going out today, she had dressed herself more conservatively than she normally would. She wasn't certain if that fact made her happy for she would present as a lady of a certain level…or horrified because she wasn't wearing her armor when she went in to treat with the enemy.

Perhaps something in the middle was the best reaction.

She smoothed her hair, drew a deep breath and headed out of

the room, down the hall to the breakfast room. It was one of the more benign of her public chambers, though even it had a large portrait of a naked woman hanging on the wall above the fire. She sighed as she walked toward the terrace doors.

She could see the Earl of Abbotton through the glass, pacing her terrace even though there was a table there with comfortable chairs that overlooked her pleasant little garden.

She stared at him while she had an unguarded moment. He had qualities that put her to mind of Benedict. They shared a broad-shouldered build and bright gray eyes that were telltale signs they were related. Beyond that, though, she had never felt they were much alike.

Derek was so stern and proper, so much a part of Society in a way Benedict never seemed to fit. He would always do the proper thing, whereas his brother…well, Benedict would more often do what was *right*, despite any consequences.

As if he sensed her watching him through the window, the Earl turned and looked directly at her. Immediately, Vivien's palms began to sweat at his stern expression, but she wiped them on her skirt and came onto the terrace with as bland a look as she could muster. She could only hope it reflected that she did not have a reaction to his unexpected presence, not that his being here made her nervous and, frankly, terrified.

"Good afternoon, my lord," she said as she closed the door behind her.

He nodded. "Miss Manning."

"I must admit, I was surprised to be told you were here. I was not expecting you—did I miss your card?" she asked, very happy that she could remain calm and polite.

He shook his head. "I should have made an appointment, I know, but I feared you would not see me."

She pursed her lips. "Despite what you think of me, Lord Abbotton, I would never be so uncouth as to refuse a meeting with you."

She might have considered it, yes, but would never have done it.

He shrugged. "I shall recall that fact for next time, Miss Manning. My most sincere apologies once again."

He looked ready to launch into whatever he was going to tell her, but Vivien interrupted him, unready for the onslaught about to come.

"Won't you sit, my lord? My staff is about to bring us tea." She motioned for the table with one hand, expecting his refusal.

He stared at the table for a long moment, then nodded. "Yes, I'll join you."

She nearly fell over in surprise. Derek had never made his distaste for her a secret, not three years ago, not now. To have him decide to break bread with her was utterly unexpected.

"V-Very good," she managed to stammer. She took her place and he joined her as the door opened and a few servants came out with tea and food. She poured him a cup, providing him with milk when he asked for it, but no sugar. She prepared her own cup and only then did he settle back and look at her evenly.

"I think we both know why I'm here today," he said.

A hundred sharp retorts balanced on her tongue, but she bit them all back. He had been polite to her thus far—there was no call for her to be otherwise.

"I assume you have come to speak to me about your brother," she offered as she took a bite of one of her cook's delicious cakes. Because of her nervousness, it tasted like sandpaper. Damn him for ruining cake.

"Yes," Derek admitted.

She arched a brow. "In fact, that is the topic of a conversation we had many years ago, isn't it? The last time you lowered yourself to darken my door."

He flinched ever so slightly at her directness, but then nodded. "Yes. I did not think I would have a need to return here and discuss this matter with you again. And yet here we are, three years past, and I feel as though I have traveled through time."

She shook her head as she thought of Benedict. The last time they had been together, she had not dared to admit her feelings, even to herself.

"No, everything is different," she said softly.

He looked at her sharply with that answer, but continued, "But it is not, Miss Manning. Just as we discussed when I came to you three years ago, my brother's well-being and future are being damaged by his obsession with you. He needs to move on. He needs to focus on the future he must fulfill." Derek sighed. "He *needs* to be free."

Vivien's own sigh caught in her throat. The Earl was not incorrect in his assessment. She knew that more than anyone. In fact she had told Benedict that very thing just a few nights ago. But Derek's attempts to intrude on the delicate situation did not please her.

"You do realize that your brother is a grown man, very intelligent and well capable of establishing his own needs," she said softly.

"On most subjects, I heartily agree with you." Derek shook his head slowly. "But on this one, I fear he is not. You are his Achilles' heel and I do not think he will, or perhaps *can,* let you go, Vivien."

She drew back at his use of her first name, as well as the fact that he would be so direct in his words. Words that pierced through her armor and made her heart swell with joy at the idea that Benedict would hold her forever.

But the joy faded at his brother's drawn, unhappy face. He was living proof that if Benedict chose her, if she gave him what he desired, it would hurt him. He would be brought low in the judgment of others, even his own family.

At first Benedict would weather that storm, but she couldn't believe it wouldn't take its toll over the years. That it wouldn't destroy their love in the long run, after he realized how much he had sacrificed for her.

"I believe you care for him," the Earl continued.

She stared, snapped from her distraction by his utterly unexpected words. "I...what?"

He smiled at her confusion. "I believe...no, I *know* you care for him. It is evident by the way you look at him, talk to him, and in the fact that you gave him up all those years ago, though it must have brought you pain."

She blinked. Was her heart so plain then? So obvious now? She had fought years to hide it, yet this man seemed to see it.

Benedict saw it.

"It did bring me pain," she admitted with great difficulty. "I don't know why I began again with him this time."

He tilted his head. "Do you not?"

She pursed her lips at his implication, but did not respond to it.

He sighed. "The facts are clear, Miss Manning, my brother will be destroyed socially if he remains with you. I don't want to see that happen."

She held his stare with great difficulty. "You mean you do not wish to be embarrassed by him or by his choices."

"No." To her surprise there was no anger in his voice or face. "No, this has nothing to do with me. I would be hurt by his regret. As would you, I imagine."

He had put her earlier thoughts into words perfectly and hearing them was a jolt of reality that pulled Vivien from whatever faint fantasies she had allowed herself of love and a future. Jolted awake, she blinked at the bright sun and the pain of reality.

"Yes," she whispered.

He nodded slowly, pained, like saying this hurt him as much as it hurt her. "Then we understand each other, I believe."

"We do," she said. "Just as we always have, I suppose."

He pushed to his feet, leaving his half-full cup and an uneaten cake behind on the plate. "Excellent. Or at least as excellent as this untenable situation could be called."

Her nod was slow and pained. "Thank you for your concern for him," she said as he smoothed his jacket. "Perhaps I had become blind to what was best over the past few weeks. But I do promise you that I will do it."

"Thank you, Miss Manning," he said and his hand came out unexpectedly toward her.

She stared for a brief second, then took his gloved hand and shook it once.

"Please be there for him once I'm…gone," she whispered.

He nodded before he headed back into her home and left her on the terrace, staring at the open door into a home that suddenly felt nothing like it.

She stepped into the parlor and rang the bell for a servant. Nettle was the first to arrive.

"Yes, miss?"

She could scarcely find her voice. "You may clear the tray," she whispered.

He stared at her a moment, as if he could sense her pain, but he said nothing about it, only nodded. "Of course, I'll have them take it right away."

"And ask Rachel to bring me my stationary," she said as she all but collapsed into the nearest chair. "I have a letter to write to my solicitor. Now, before I find a reason to change my mind."

Benedict paced the parlor in his mother's townhome, restless and anxious as he awaited her arrival. Being called here, just a few days after his last encounter with Vivien, gave him no relief. In fact, it only made his entire emotional state that much worse.

His mind was clouded with thoughts, with memories, with frustrations he could no longer ignore. How many times could he declare his love only to have it denied…or worse, ignored. This was the second time he had done so with similar results.

The first time he told Vivien he loved her, it had been foolish and he knew it. She had made it clear she could not be with him and in his desperation he had blurted out the truth. As expected, she had recoiled and their relationship had swiftly ended afterward.

But this time…well, things had changed. *She* had changed. They were closer than ever and he thought, for a brief moment, that she had come to care for him. Love him.

In truth, he still believed that. She did care for him, he had sensed that dozens of times since they were brought back together with such unexpected intensity. And yet something held her back.

Something kept her from being able to accept him.

But what? He kept racking his mind, trying to find the source of her hesitance, her desperation, the distance she kept between them even as her eyes brightened with emotion around him. But there was nothing, nothing except the same old questions that had been plaguing them for years.

The door to the parlor opened and Benedict scrambled to his feet as his mother unexpectedly entered the room.

She was a tall, slender woman, with eyes like his and his brother's. She had always been beautiful, a Diamond of the First Water her first Season when she caught the eye of their father. They had married within that year and somehow, over the time they spent together, had developed a love match made of deep affection and respect.

His father's loss had taken its toll on his mother, but she was beginning to come out of her grief and regain some of the sparkle and shine that made her unique.

"Benedict," she said, holding out her hands in greeting.

He crossed the room to her and took her gloved fingers. She turned her cheek so he could press a kiss on the smooth surface and then backed away. She had never been overly demonstrative in her affection, though he knew she loved her children greatly. But she was proper.

"Mama, you look well," he said as he allowed her to take a seat on her favorite chair and then found a place on the settee across from her.

She shrugged. "I need a new maid. Isabel is leaving and she's begun knotting my hair as she thinks of her future husband rather than my needs."

"I actually know of a few servants who will need new positions soon."

Benedict smiled. Their plan for Dersingham had worked in spades. The Earl was utterly ruined, his own wife had left to stay with her mother and the women who had once been tortured by him were beginning to find new places of employment, thanks to a little help from Benedict and some friends. Vivien would be pleased about that, at least.

"Good. Have your servants send a list and I'll make some inquiries." His mother arched a brow. "And what about you, son? You say I look well, but you do not."

He stifled a chuckle. "Direct, as always, Mama."

She shrugged. "Why shouldn't I be direct, especially when it comes to those I love? You look tired."

"I am tired," he admitted.

"I hope this isn't because of that woman," his mother said with a sniff.

Benedict jerked his gaze to her with wide eyes. "W-Woman?" he repeated.

She arched a brow. "Please don't treat me like one of those simpering fools who pretend not to know anything. I know you've taken back up with that woman. What is her name again? Vivien or Violet or something else with a V? For vulgar, no doubt."

He swallowed hard. This was a most indelicate topic and one he had never imagined he would be openly discussing with his mother, of all people. But then again, perhaps it had not been brought to her attention by a stranger.

"Derek must be very desperate indeed, if he brought you into such an indecent subject," he said, gritting his teeth with every word.

She shook her head. "You needn't get your feathers ruffled at your brother. He has said nothing to me. You think we ladies do not hear about the antics of the gentlemen? We simply have the control not to bring it up."

He stared at her. "Then why bring it up now?"

"I had no desire to do so, I assure you. In fact, I have tried to ignore it, but the situation has begun to get out of hand," she said with a sigh. "It is one thing to have an affair or to obtain a mistress, but it is another to ignore your duties in order to keep the company of that lady. How do you think our Prince became a laughing stock?"

"My duties are fulfilled," he said, though his voice croaked.

She shook her head. "You told me you intended to look for a bride this Season. I was thrilled to hear it. Your brother has married and I'm certain that he will begin producing heirs in good time, but you are still his spare. If something happens or if he is only able to have daughters, you will be obligated to create heirs to carry on the family name."

"So all this is about heirs?" he repeated, overcome with disbelief even though Derek had said as much during their last encounter.

"You can be terribly modern about all this and pretend that your father's name doesn't matter, but it does," his mother snapped. "I owe it to him to ensure it carries on. And in all honesty, I think settling down with a lady of proper value would be good for you. You have been...*unpredictable* as of late and it troubles me. I've always believed I could depend on you."

He clenched his hands as he tried with all his might to retain some civility. "So you think that by involving myself with someone outside the realm of your approval, this somehow proves I'm not dependable?"

She shrugged one slender shoulder. "It could create problems for me, for your brother, for yourself if you got carried away and believed yourself in love with this person. Or are my reports incorrect?"

He pursed his lips. "I do not think I want to discuss that with you, Mama."

She held his stare for a long moment and then tilted her head. "Very well. You say that you can handle yourself and I have no choice but to have faith in you. But that does not mean I cannot encourage you. So I have made a list."

Benedict squeezed his eyes shut. "A list," he repeated with as much pain in his voice as he felt deep in his soul.

"Of women currently on the market who would be the most appropriate matches for you," his mother said as she dug into her reticule to pull out a folded sheet of vellum.

As he watched her, Benedict had a flash to something very familiar. A memory of being in Vivien's chamber and seeing a list of hers on her end table. Her reaction had been powerful and she had snatched the paper away before he could read anything on it beyond the words in the title that read "Loose Ends".

"Benedict," his mother said, her tone sharp as she shook the paper in front of his face until he took it. He looked at the neat line of names, almost two dozen, but could hardly focus as his mind returned again and again to Vivien and *her* mysterious list.

Why had she wanted to hide it from him? Did her reaction have something to do with her behavior in the weeks since that night?

"Are you not even going to pretend to examine the names I have so carefully compiled?" his mother asked.

He glanced at her. Her arms were folded and one slippered foot tapped beneath her gown. He shook thoughts of Vivien away as best he could.

"Of course," he said, looking at her chosen names with a little more focus. But even as he scanned them with increasing dread, he knew one thing above all others.

He needed to find Vivien's secret list. And he would.

CHAPTER 21

Vivien sat in the parlor of Mariah's home, nervousness building inside her with every tick of the clock. Today was a regular meeting of the Charitable Fund for Young Ladies and her friends went about their discussions as normal. For the past hour, she had remained almost entirely silent, watching the two women interact, smile at each other, look over paperwork together as they discussed the best idea for this problem or a way to promote their cause to ladies of rank.

She would miss this terribly.

Suddenly Mariah turned on her. "Vivien, I cannot remain silent any longer."

Vivien tensed. Her intelligent friend was about to comment on her distance, and then she would be forced to tell them something she dreaded.

"What in the world did you do to Lord Dersingham?" she finished with a laugh.

"You mean his sudden change of fortune?" Vivien said, her lips twitching with laughter she could scarcely hold in.

That was one of the high moments as of late. Dersingham had been crushed under the weight of his scandal when the engagement to the American had failed and his creditors began to call in their debts. He was no longer invited to parties and had been holed up in his London estate for days without word.

"Change in fortune is one way to put it," Mariah said with an arched brow. "The man is utterly destroyed. They say he will never be invited back to polite Society again and now women are coming out of the woodwork to accuse him of impropriety. There may even be an investigation by the Crown about a recent duel and a stolen bit of gold… Since all these circumstances happened just a few days after you brought up his evil deeds, I *must* think you had a hand in it."

"I have heard even his servants are fleeing the house, seeking and finding new employment in the best homes in all of London," Lysandra continued with a wide smile. "Thanks to you?"

She shrugged with relief. The inevitable was put off for the time being.

"I suppose I had some hand in the fact that the American won't marry his son as planned, which stole the funds right from the bastard's coffers, but the rest is not my doing at all. It is only a fair recompense for years of evil deeds. And Benedict has ensured the safe placement of the servants from Dersingham's home, not me."

Lysandra held her gaze for a long moment. "Benedict is a good man."

She couldn't smile. It was too painful. "Indeed he is."

"Isn't there any way to be with him?" Lysandra pressed.

Vivien swallowed. She wasn't even going to deny that was her heart's desire. "No. Not with my reputation."

"But Lysandra and I each came from similar backgrounds and our husbands—" Mariah began.

Vivien lifted a hand to stop her. "You did not come from anything like my background. Lysandra never had a lover beyond her husband and you married a rake with a terrible reputation who could be expected to do something so shocking. Neither of you were ever the most notorious woman in the city."

Lysandra worried her lip. "When you say that, it is so unkind to yourself. You are far more than just a mistress or a woman of a certain reputation. Your work with the charitable fund proves that."

"And I appreciate that you both see me as more than what I am," Vivien sighed. "But it is to no end. I cannot be with Benedict. It would destroy him and I…I care too much about him to live with those kinds of consequences for him. There is nothing else to be said about it."

"I disagree," Mariah said with a shrug. "There is a great deal more to be said."

Vivien drew in a breath. She could sit all day with her friends, debating this subject. But there was one way to cease their ramblings on her love for Benedict.

"Perhaps there *is* more to be said," Vivien conceded as she pushed to her feet and walked to the window. She couldn't look at them when she told them the truth. "There are plans to be made, you see."

"Plans?" Lysandra repeated with confusion.

She nodded but couldn't turn. Not until she had confessed. "I—I am leaving London."

Silence greeted her statement and she finally pivoted on her heel and looked at them. They were staring at her, neither one completely understanding.

"On a holiday?" Mariah offered.

Vivien's breath caught. The words caught in her throat far more than she ever imagined they would, especially when Lysandra's hands had begun to shake and Mariah seemed so utterly perplexed by the very idea.

"No. I mean never to return. I am *leaving* London for good."

Mariah shoved away from her chair, flipping it over in the process as she staggered to her feet. "What?"

Vivien bit her lip. Her friend, her best friend, was trembling, her eyes filling with sudden tears.

"Please don't make me say it a third time."

Mariah shook her head and Lysandra slowly joined both women on their feet. Normally she was the sweetest one, the most innocent and the most emotional. But at that moment, she seemed utterly calm.

"Why are you leaving?" she asked. She reached for Mariah and took her hand, squeezing it for comfort when the two women faced Vivien as a united front.

Vivien sighed. She'd created so many stories in her mind of how she would tell her friends this news…if she told them at all. But right now, only the truth could make them see why this was not just a choice, but an imperative.

"I am in love with Benedict Greystone," she admitted, every word stinging like fire across her heart. "But we cannot be together." Lysandra drew a breath to protest, but Vivien shook her head. "Please do not argue, my dear, you cannot understand how much more painful your attempts to change my mind make this."

Lysandra snapped her lips shut, pink darkening her skin.

"But why not just part with him, then, and stay in London as you have for nearly a decade?" Mariah asked in a shaky voice.

She shook her head. "On the night of my birthday, I realized something I had been denying for years," Vivien explained. "I am not happy in this life anymore. In fact, I am very empty."

Lysandra drew back. "I had no idea."

Vivien shrugged. "Your ignorance was of my design. But as there is no way I could ever start again here, where my face and name are so well-known, I realized that in order to make a new life for myself, I have no choice but to leave."

"You made this decision the night of your birthday and you said nothing until now?" Mariah blinked in utter disbelief. "Not even to us?"

Vivien drew in a shaky breath. "I made a list of things I must do, loose ends I must settle before I could depart London. You and Lysandra were very high on that list, I assure you. Celebrating you, spending time with you, letting you both know how loved and cherished your friendship has been to me over the years."

Lysandra gasped as the first tears began to fall. "But you denied us that same time. Here we have been taking the hours we spent for granted, believing there would be hundreds, thousands more in a lifetime to share."

Vivien shook her head. She could see she had hurt them and that had never been her intention.

"I'm so sorry. It is not in my nature to be open, to share my thoughts or my pains. To be truthful, I was afraid of your reaction, afraid you would try to convince me to stay here."

"*Can* we convince you?" Mariah pleaded, her tears now sliding down her cheeks in waterfalls.

Vivien considered the question. In this moment, with the two women sobbing at the thought of her loss, it was easy to imagine there was some way to work it out. To remain in London and forget her unhappiness, her emptiness, to ignore the loss of Benedict and watch him marry with a false smile on her face.

The very thought made her chest feel hollow and her stomach turn. And proved that even the love of her friends could not erase or change the love of this one man.

"No," she whispered, blinking at her own tears. "I'm afraid this is a decision I must make. I'll be destroyed if I stay."

Lysandra nodded, but Vivien knew she would. She was too sweet of temper not to let someone she loved go if they felt it was best for them. Mariah was another story. Jaded like Vivien, though not as completely, the two women had been close for years. And Mariah was far more likely to hate her for her choices.

Her friend slowly crossed the room toward her, pale face unreadable even as she moved just inches from Vivien. For a moment, she only looked at her, then Mariah tugged her in for a fierce hug.

"I would never ask you to do something that would cause you pain. If you must leave, then I have no choice but to understand," her friend whispered into her hair as the two women clung to each other.

Vivien motioned Lysandra to join them and for a moment, they stood, arms around each other, crying in unison. Until Vivien pulled away with a laugh.

"All right, you ninnies, that is enough," she said, laughing through her tears. "I shall not ruin my reputation of being a cold, ruthless woman by sobbing over you."

Mariah chuckled. "No one would ever ask you to."

"When will you leave?" Lysandra asked, retaking her seat and wiping her eyes with a handkerchief she produced from some mysterious fold of her gown.

Vivien took a seat and frowned. "I had planned to spend a final Season here, celebrating my life and leaving an impression no one could forget, but now...now I think it would be best for me to quietly disappear soon. I have already procured a home on the continent that my solicitor says can be ready in a week. My staff has begun to catalog my things so that I can arrange for the removal of what I wish to take with me."

"And what of the house?" Mariah asked. "Will you sell it?"

"There is a reason I brought this subject up during our meeting," Vivien said with a smile. "You see, one of my items on my list of things to do before I left the city was to give away that which I don't need. And I do not need that house any longer."

Lysandra shook her head. "I don't understand."

"I would like to donate it to the cause we have created together," Vivien explained. "I think you two could make it a place where women in dire straits can come and live safely. Can you imagine if abused servants felt as if they had a safe alternative to staying in their situations? Or a woman carrying the shame of a child out of wedlock, forced upon her by a so-called gentleman, had a home she could run to? In short, turn my house of sin into a safe haven."

Mariah shook her head, but her wide smile told Vivien she approved even before she spoke. "It is an amazing idea! But are you certain you won't want to return to the house? Once it has been transformed, it can never go back."

Vivien smiled. "That is the idea. For the house and for me."

Lysandra let out a long sigh. "Then it is settled."

"Yes." Vivien said, but in the end the issue felt anything but. Telling her friends was a huge part, and lessened her guilt over keeping the secret even more.

But there was one person who was still in the dark about her plans. And she had no idea how to tell Benedict that it was time to let her go…this time permanently.

CHAPTER 22

Benedict stood in the foyer of Vivien's house, looking around in an attempt to see with new eyes. Now that he was focused on what could drive her to push him away, what could make her so afraid to embrace what she knew he could offer…all he could see were those reasons.

Vivien had made money in her life. From recent research, he knew that her first protector had settled her very well. A second had assisted her with investing the proceeds and given her an additional sum. A third gifted her with this home and suddenly a woman tossed out by her family after an assault had been transformed into an independent woman who moved in influential circles.

Was it that which kept her from him? Her independence? Though he was certain she had concerns about surrendering the life she had built, that didn't ring true. Independence would not create desperation.

"Good afternoon, sir," Nettle intoned as he entered the foyer. "I am sorry I wasn't here to greet you myself, but we weren't expecting you. I'm certain the footman who answered the door told you that Miss Manning is not currently available for guests."

Benedict shook his questions aside and prepared to play a role.

"Ah, do not trouble yourself, Nettle. I interrupted the staff's luncheon, I realize, and you are correct that I was not invited nor expected. But you see, I wanted to plan a special evening for Miss Manning."

Nettle lifted his eyebrows slightly, but Benedict could see the approval in the servant's eyes. Old Nettle had always been a good and dedicated man. It was too bad Benedict had to trade on those qualities to obtain a sliver of truth from the woman he loved.

"I see," Nettle said. "And does this mean you wish access to her chambers, even though she is not home at present?"

Benedict nodded. "It does. A few nights ago, I spent time in her *real* chambers. Those are the ones I wish to access."

Nettle's face, which had been open with readiness to approve the request, now fell.

"Sir—" he began, tone polite yet firm with impending refusal.

"Ah, before you refuse me, I realize this is not a common request," Benedict interrupted, playing his good-natured attitude very carefully. Nettle was suspicious and protective already—he would be too easy to set off and then Benedict would have nothing.

"No, sir," Nettle responded.

"But the fact that I know of her chambers and have been in them, even spent an evening in them with her…that is uncommon as well, is it not?"

The butler shifted and Benedict could see his discomfort. Despite all he'd seen, the man remained uncomfortable with such direct references to his employer's lifestyle.

"I only wish to do something for her," Benedict pressed, and in that he was not lying.

She would be very angry when she saw he'd pried, but he wanted to be there for her. And he had to know the truth before he could make a case for that.

"Since you have been in her chamber before, I will allow it," Nettle said slowly, his uncertainty still clear. "Do you require any assistance from the staff?"

"No," Benedict said swiftly. "I will be able to prepare the room myself, thank you. You should return to your luncheon."

Nettle glanced behind him toward the kitchen and the servant quarters through the door and down the hall. Benedict could see the longing in the other man's stare. Vivien's cook was known to be a marvel and the servant fare likely reflected that.

"Miss Manning's maid was tidying her room just before luncheon," he said. "And her chamber door is unlocked. You may proceed there."

"Very good," Benedict called after the man as he gave a smart bow and headed back to his lunch.

He chuckled and moved for the stairs. With the servants at their meal, it was quiet in the house and he moved without concern about who was watching.

At the door to Vivien's chamber, he hesitated. Once he went inside, there would be no altering the violation of privacy he was about to commit. He could only hope it would be worth her wrath later.

He pushed open the door and went inside.

The bed was freshly made and the windows had been opened by Vivien's maid so that a soft, flower-scented breeze came in from the garden outside. Sunlight hit every corner of the chamber, filling it with light and beauty.

He drew in a long breath and walked to the end table beside her bed where he had first seen the list. He doubted it remained in the vicinity, but it was as good a place to start his journey as any. He lifted the book and opened her drawer, but there was nothing to be found there beyond a pair of spectacles he'd never seen her wear but could be for reading.

He put everything back in its place and sighed. The room was spacious, with many places to hide something in the many drawers and crevices in this space and her adjoining dressing room.

He got to his feet and began to search. As he opened drawers and peeked into armoires, a feeling of unease crept over him. He was truly violating her trust by doing this and with every passing moment, he felt worse and worse about that undeniable fact.

And yet he was driven to complete the distasteful task. He was obsessed with the truth and somehow he knew that it would be found on the neatly written paper he'd caught a glimpse of a short time ago.

But would it be worth it?

He wasn't certain of that answer. And he was still questioning that fact when he sat down at her dressing table to continue his search. It was a small table with a mirror which had a lamp on either side of it. Bottles of perfume, brushes and combs were laid out neatly on the table's surface and a hidden set of doors on one side of the table revealed a kohl pencil and a few pink powders, perhaps for lips or cheeks.

He sighed as he shut the hidden doors. There was a second set of them on the opposite side and he opened them to find a jewelry box in the hidden cubby within. He wrinkled his brow. In his search, he had determined that Vivien had transformed an old armoire into an elaborate display case for her massive collection of jewelry. Both paste and very real pieces hung from hooks and draped over velvet displays.

"Why do you need this little box, then, Vivien?" he asked the room at large as he drew it out and set it on the top of the dressing table. There was a latch on the front of the box and he unhooked it, holding his breath as he opened the top to find…

Nothing of consequence. There were a few miniatures of her mother and a man he supposed was her late father. It also contained one very inexpensive and plain ring that he also believed to be from the life she had abandoned in Sapsgate and a paper that was a copy of the deed of this house.

He frowned as he flipped the box shut in frustration. What if the information he sought wasn't here at all? What if Vivien had destroyed it or carried it with her on her person while she went out to see her friends today?

Or what if that list had been nothing of importance at all and had been tossed away with other household lists of things to buy and do for the mundane daily runnings of the estate?

"Damn it," he muttered. He grabbed for the box and was about to shove it back into the cubby and reevaluate his decision to come here at all when something caught his eye.

When he'd slammed the lid shut, the box had shimmied and now there was a faint corner of a piece of paper peeking up from the cloth backing of the box itself.

He turned the box slowly. The fabric backing had been cheaply attached to the wooden surface with a series of small, rusty nails. It took nothing for him to gently tug and loosen two at the corner exactly where the piece of paper made itself known.

He folded the cloth back and tugged at the folded sheet hidden within. With a bit of turning and pulling, it popped free. He pushed the box away and stared at what he had found. He had no idea if this was the list he sought, but if Vivien had gone to all the trouble of hiding it, she must consider it highly private.

A part of him told him to put it away, leave her chamber and offer her an apology for his actions. But a larger part, the part which loved her and desperately wanted to find proof that he could be with her, screamed louder at him to open it.

He listened to the second half and gently opened the paper.

She had torn the sheet away before he could read it before, but this was definitely the paper he had found in her chamber before. On it he found a list of ten items titled *Loose Ends to Tie Before Departing London*. His heart sank as he stared at the title. And it sank even further as he realized his name was the last item. Just after one word that stabbed his heart:

Disappear.

~

Vivien swept through the front door, past Nettle. She handed over her gloves and wrap.

"Good afternoon, Miss Vivien," he said, his eyes darting toward the stairs.

She wrinkled her brow. Her butler seemed a bit distracted. "Good afternoon, Nettle. Are there any cards?"

"A few," he said slowly, reaching for the tray beside the door.

She examined it. "Excellent, there are less than half the usual amount. I suppose that means the masses are finally beginning to understand the meaning of my silence."

She took the stack and smiled at her butler as she moved toward the parlor. To her surprise, Nettle trailed after her.

"P-Perhaps you would like to take your tea upstairs in your private chambers?" he suggested.

She looked at each card and invitation and tossed them into a pile to be refused and discarded. There was nothing there to tempt her and she had a great many plans to make, including telling her servants the truth and helping them arrange new employment.

"No," she finally responded. "I don't think I'll have tea this afternoon. Our lunch was very rich and I am full. But I do want to take a walk in the gardens, so I'll finish my business and do that. Thank you, Nettle."

She said the last as a dismissal, but her butler did not move from the doorway.

She lifted her gaze to him in confusion. He gently shifted his weight from one foot to another as he stared at her and then back over his shoulder as if he were expecting someone.

"What is it?" she asked with a shake of her head. "Why this strange behavior, Nettle? Has something happened? The staff is well, are they not?"

He nodded. "Oh yes, Miss, the staff is quite well, but you see...I... you have a visitor, Miss Manning."

Vivien groaned. There was no one she wished to see, especially since from Nettle's behavior it was likely an unpleasant intruder who had refused to accept she was not at home.

She tossed the remaining cards aside. "And where is this visitor if not in the main parlor? The terrace? The library?"

He shook his head. "No miss, he is in your chamber."

Her lips parted. Nettle would never allow an unknown man into her bedroom, nor one with which she had shared a history but no longer saw. In fact, the only man she believed capable of talking his way past the front of Nettle was Benedict.

She swallowed. "Mr. Greystone?" she asked.

Her servant nodded. "I'm sorry, miss. He arrived in the midst of the servant luncheon and asked to prepare a surprise for you. I agreed, but in the time he has been here he has not once gone to a carriage for arrangements or flowers. In fact, he has not made a peep from the chamber at all."

Vivien shook her head. No doubt he was sprawled naked on the bed in her public chamber, waiting to seduce her and end the distance that had separated them since he'd declared his love for her.

And in truth, that didn't sound so bad. She could spend an afternoon making love to him. Saying goodbye, though he would not necessarily know her intention. She would far rather have their last encounter be one of passion than of anger.

"I see. Well, I will handle him, Nettle," she said as she moved up the stairs. "I assume he is in the public chamber?"

Her butler hesitated and she stopped to look back at him. Nettle's face was deathly pale. "I—I allowed him access to your private rooms, Miss Vivien."

Vivien squeezed her eyes shut. So their last encounter was to be in her real room. She nodded.

"Don't trouble yourself, Nettle. I, more than anyone, know that Mr. Greystone can be remarkably persuasive. I will ring if we have need of anything."

She continued up the stairs and down the hall. With a deep

breath, she pushed open her chamber door, expecting to find Benedict awaiting her in some erotic pose.

Instead, she found him seated in a chair he had moved to face the door. He was completely clothed and his expression was anything but seductive. It was hard, angry, broken.

In his hand, he held a sheet of paper. As she stepped inside, he lifted it up and turned it, revealing it to be the very list she had written about leaving London. She staggered as she stared at the proof of her future, her actions...the proof of how far he had been willing to go to unearth the truth.

CHAPTER 23

"How could you?" Vivien burst out as she rushed into the room and snatched the paper from Benedict's hand. She held it to her chest, but there was no protecting the information now. He had seen it all.

"How could *I*?" he repeated, popping up to his feet and pivoting on her. "You are leaving London?"

She swallowed. "Yes," she admitted softly.

What little color remained in his cheeks blanched away, as if he had held out hope that her list was counterfeit, but now he had to fully face the truth.

"When did you plan to tell me?" he whispered.

She shifted. "I just did."

He shook his head. "Only after I was forced to ransack your room looking for evidence. If I hadn't found this list and confronted you, when did you intend to tell me you were leaving?"

She squeezed her eyes shut. She was bombarded by so many emotions—anger at him for his invasion of her privacy, guilt that she had lied to him, pain that this was to be their final encounter rather than something loving and pleasant.

But now that it was happening, she knew that honesty was her only weapon.

She looked at him, though holding his gaze was so difficult that it physically hurt her. "I would not have told you," she admitted. "When I was gone, I would have left a letter to be delivered to you."

He staggered back, clutching at the chair closest to him. The betrayal in his eyes was palpable.

"When?" he asked after a moment that seemed to stretch forever. "Because there are only three items left to be completed on that list. Give away what you don't need, my name and disappear."

She swallowed. "Actually, I finished giving away what I didn't need this very afternoon. I have let a house on the continent and I intend to depart for it within a fortnight. My solicitor is making arrangements for my travel. I intended to tell my servants the truth this week and help them obtain new positions. Then leave."

He only stared at her as she continued talking, shaking his head with disbelief with her every word. "You have put so much thought into this."

She nodded. "I had to, Benedict. I am changing my life, changing everything."

"You are running *again*," he accused with a brutal snap to his tone that made her turn her face away from it.

"I am not running," she whispered.

"Bollocks," he barked as he moved on her. He didn't touch her, but he was almost pressed against her as he said, "Ten years ago, you ran from your family."

"I had no choice."

"Perhaps not, but you also did not wish to face the difficulty presented there. And now you intend to run again. As if reinventing yourself will change what you have done or seen or what you feel!"

"You mean it won't change that I am a whore," she said, staring at him and daring him to say that wasn't what he meant with his angry words.

To her surprise, he immediately issued that denial. "The only one of the two of us who believes you are a whore is you," he said. "What I mean is that when your emotions get too high, you believe you can leave them behind. That by changing your name and address that you can forget the pain. But you've already proven you can't. The pain is part of what makes us who we are, Vivien."

She stepped away. "A fact you know nothing about. You will find a bride this Season or next, Benedict. You will start over and be allowed to do so. I won't. If I remain in London, I will always be seen by those around me as a mistress, a whore. I could never be anything else and I want so much to be."

He didn't immediately respond, but stared at her. "What do you want to be?" he finally asked.

"I—" she began, then hesitated.

She stared into the eyes of this man. He was angry, yes, but there was so much love there. So much desire for something more than she had ever allowed them to have.

"I want to be me," she whispered. "Not what my parents wanted, not what I was forced to become due to circumstances. Just me."

He reached out and briefly touched her face. "The goal is a worthy one."

She smiled but then reality hit her again and she pulled away. "But not here. Benedict, you must let me go."

"Why?" he pressed.

She threw up her hands in frustration. "For a hundred reasons you know as well as I do! Because you belong in London, because you are a gentleman and I am most definitely not a lady, because there would be a scandal if you made a life with me, because you would lose your family if I was your choice, even if your brother says he would not cut you off…"

"My brother?" he repeated.

She immediately wished she could take back the words, especially as understanding began to dawn in his gray eyes.

"What does Derek have to do with anything? And when did the two of you talk about me?"

She swallowed. "You are a lucky man, Benedict. You have a family who loves you, enough to try to protect you. Even from your own foolish inclinations. If your brother ever intervened—"

He squeezed his eyes shut. "He intervened…of course, why did I not see it before? He spoke to you and that set you on this path."

"No," she said with raised hands. "I decided to change my life before you and I were even together again. Your brother has no bearing on my leaving London."

"Then when did he talk to you?" he asked.

She folded her arms. If she told him the truth, the truth about three years ago, the truth about three *days* ago, he would be destroyed. His relationship with his family would be destroyed. She could not do that to him.

"Please, my dearest," she soothed. "Let this go. Let me go and we will call this time together what it was, a stolen moment that could never last."

He stared at her. "It was before this latest affair of ours, wasn't it?" he asked, breathless with disbelief. "He spoke to you when I was your protector three years ago."

She pressed her lips together, but she could think of no lie that he would believe. "Yes. He spoke to me, we talked of how tangled up you were in your love for me."

"That bastard!" Benedict slammed his hand against the closest tabletop and the items on it shivered with the force.

"I already felt the same way as he did, Benedict," she pleaded. "I saw that our affiliation had to end. He never threatened me, he never bribed me. He *asked* me to let you go."

"And you were more than willing to do so," he said, his voice suddenly icy cold.

She stared at him. "I died that day, watching you walk away in pain. Knowing we would never again be together. God help me, I was weak and I ran back to you in these past weeks, but leaving again is the right thing to do."

"According to my brother?" he asked.

She hesitated. "Right is right—it does not matter who points it out."

He nodded and paced away from her. For a long time, he was silent, staring out her window to her gardens, breathing in and out with shallow, shaking breaths.

"Perhaps you are right that Derek means well," he finally said, turning toward her. "And that you are only doing this in order to protect me."

She nodded. It seemed that perhaps he was ready to be reasonable.

Except he didn't look reasonable as he moved on her a step.

"But I never asked for your protection. Yes, if I marry you, I would be shunned from good Society in London. And," he continued, "it is very likely that my mother would show her disapproval by cutting me off, at least for some amount of time. She might never accept you, for her propriety is a part of her that is bone-deep. I believe Jocelyn would be kind to you in private, but in public she could never acknowledge you. These things are facts, and I am not so stupid as you and my brother think I am that I do not realize they are true."

She flinched. He had to admit these things, this was an excellent first step, but, oh, how those words stung.

He gently cupped her shoulders and pulled her closer. "But what you and my brother failed to consider, what you have always failed to ask me, is whether or not I care."

She sucked in a breath. "You *think* you would not care, but in time—"

"Do you know how much I *hate* Society?" he asked. "Living by their rules, marrying for status, pretending to like someone because their title is higher than yours…it has never given me pleasure and it never will. If I do as you and my brother ask of me, I will be respectable and miserable. *In time*, as you put it, I will despise my Society-approved wife and heirs. I will drink myself into a pickled state and probably die by drowning in my bathtub, which will be very undignified."

She didn't want to smile, but she did. "You overstate it."

"Do I? It is just as possible an outcome to the one you assume, which is that I would marry you and end up regretting not being invited to parties at Lady Frickenbottom's house."

"There is no Lady Frickenbottom," Vivien insisted with a shake of her head.

He shrugged. "You know what I mean. None of us can tell the future, my dear. There is only one thing I know and I know it more than I have ever known anything in my life."

Vivien swallowed and her voice cracked. "What is that?"

"I love you. And you love me."

She stared. Confronted directly by the facts she could no longer deny, she couldn't think of something to say. She turned slightly, trying to escape his arms.

"That is two things," she muttered.

He shook his head and held fast to her. "It is one. We love each other, Vivien. Can you not see how powerful that fact is? Not one couple in a thousand, in ten thousand, has the kind of love we do. Throwing it away is a reckless, selfish act. Running from it will never allow you to escape it. Trust me, I tried. When you left me, I did everything I could to crush the love I felt. If you do the same, it will only fester and infect everything in your life. But once you embrace it, it brightens everything. It elevates the mundane to the amazing."

She reached up to cup his cheeks. He seemed so certain that she could almost believe him. Except the consequences of his request loomed so large in her mind that they pushed at all other thoughts.

"Admitting, accepting that love as you say may very well do all you suggest, but our love also has the power to destroy. Destroy *you*. You have said it yourself. And that would destroy me."

He moved away. "You are determined to start a new life, away from London?"

She nodded even as tears began to spill down her cheeks. "It is the only way."

He sighed and her stomach clenched at his expression. Despite his beautiful declaration, he was going to let her go.

"You are probably right. Leaving is the best answer for you, to find yourself, to find acceptance."

She nodded as she backed away, beginning the painful process of parting from him forever. "I'm glad you understand. You will forget me soon enough, I know. Whatever else you think, that will be true."

He wrinkled his brow. "Oh no, that will never happen."

She shook her head. "I—I don't understand."

"No, you wouldn't." He smiled like she was a child. "You don't believe in devotion because it terrifies you. In time you will. Vivien, I am not letting you go with my blessing. I am coming with you."

She blinked. "I—what?"

He laughed at her confusion. "You must leave London and I accept that. But I cannot live without you again. I have tried and it is remarkably unpleasant. So I will go with you. We will change our names and buy our house on the continent and explore museums and create a life that will free us both from the constraints that have long held us down."

"You could not leave your family," she insisted.

He sighed. "My family does love me. I know you are correct on that score. And I have to have faith that someday, when their disappointment has faded, perhaps they will accept me again, accept you. But when I consider leaving them behind or being left behind by you, there is only one choice."

"Benedict—"

"Make a new family with me, Vivien. One we will love with all our hearts."

She could not speak. Not when he was saying such lovely, lovely things.

He moved closer and finally his arms came around her. "If you leave, I will follow you. I will find you in every city you run to until you are forced to accept me. Do yourself a favor and avoid all that upheaval. Take me with you on your adventures."

He was smiling but his eyes were serious. He meant what he said. He was not letting her go this time. And her reaction at this heavy-handed refusal to accept her choices, much to her surprise, was joy. Excitement.

"Benedict, you would be throwing away everything that matters," she whispered, still reticent to steal him from his life.

He shook his head. "Have I not made myself clear? *You* are what matters. Perhaps it will take a few years to prove that to you. But I'm willing to work hard at making you believe. At coaxing you to accept that you love me."

She blinked. "You think I must be coaxed? No, I know I love you. I accepted that, though reluctantly, shortly after we began this second affair."

He blinked and there was such a wash of relief and joy on his face that she nearly stumbled at the sight of it.

"You are willing to admit you love me?" he repeated.

She nodded. "I love you, Benedict. And that has been very hard for me to realize when I knew I would leave you."

His face reflected sudden understanding. "That was why you had such desperation. Such pain."

She nodded. "Because I loved you and I knew we were bound to lose each other."

"But we aren't. Losing each other is a *choice*, Vivien, and I refuse to make it. So what will it be? Will you force me to follow you from country to country, dodging the dangers of Napoleon as I declare my undying affection in ways that would put a novel to shame...or will you surrender now and allow me to love you the way you should be loved? Forever."

Vivien swallowed. What he was asking for was the ultimate leap of faith. But not just for her...for him, as well. They would both lose something in the gamble in order to gain something far greater.

She reached out and took his hand. "May we love *each other* the way we *both* deserved to be loved instead? It seems to be a more equal exchange."

He laughed. "You have always been a born negotiator. And the answer is yes."

She smiled. For the first time since she was a girl, she looked at the future and felt joy and excitement, terror and bliss, all rolled into one. And for the first time ever, she knew she had a partner to share it all with.

"Then may I show you our new home?" she asked, moving to the closet and the plans she had hidden there. "Unless you already found these?"

He laughed as she laid the sketches and information out in front of him. "No, not yet. But I cannot wait to see the future we will share."

He moved to examine the paperwork, but she caught his chin with her fingers. As she moved in for a kiss, all her fears, all her pain melted away. All she felt was love. All she would ever feel was love.

EPILOGUE

Four years later

The soft blue waters of the Mediterranean swished onto the sand and tickled Vivien's toes. She laughed as she curled closer to Benedict's warm body and watched as her three-year-old daughter danced in the surf, holding hands with Lysandra and Andrew's son, just a few months older than she.

Mariah took John's hand. "I see a love match in the future."

The six friends laughed together and a swell of joy lifted through Vivien's body. It was a common feeling, one she had experienced hundreds of times since she left London and embarked on her new life with Benedict.

She had wanted to change her name, but he had convinced her otherwise. And while they had occasionally run into people who knew her past, especially in the very large cities, being Vivien Greystone had been a true joy.

"I cannot believe this holiday is the first time we have spent together since your departure," Lysandra said as she waved to the governesses who were wrangling the children.

"Much has changed since then," Vivien said with a nod. "We've both had children, Mariah is going to have her own in a few months."

Mariah cast a quick glance at John and everyone could see how giddy with pleasure he was at the prospect of a child.

"Somehow we all became respectable," Mariah laughed.

Vivien smiled, but as Benedict lifted her fingers to his lips, their eyes met and any respectability she felt faded and was replaced by a desire that never faded, no matter the number of years they had been married. In the end, she was still this man's lover and his love. Time had proven she could be both and she had never been so happy she had taken the risk he proposed when he all but forced this future on her years before.

"So tell me the news," Vivien pressed. "Is there anything to report from our old friends in London?"

"I have news, but not of a friend," Mariah said.

Vivien sat up straighter. "Who?"

"Dersingham is dead," Lysandra provided as she motioned the children to come in from the warm, Italian waters.

Vivien and Benedict exchanged a look. "Dead?" he repeated.

"Yes, died an utter pauper, locked in an asylum after he made an attempt on a very young girl." Mariah shuddered. "Once he was revealed by you two, his entire life collapsed. His son seems to be making a very valiant attempt to repair the damage. I have heard he is a fair master to his servants and he has even donated to the Charitable Society."

"I'm happy to hear that the sins of the father do not necessarily have to be visited upon the sons." Benedict pushed to his feet. "Speaking of which, I must go catch our daughter before she frightens the dog to death."

The other men also got to their feet and wandered off toward the blue water and the racing children.

"And speaking of the Charitable Society," Lysandra added as they watched their husbands in the distance, "our home is running so smoothly. The women are grateful and their lives are truly changed by your generosity, Vivien."

Vivien smiled. "It is something I am so pleased by," she admitted. "That life seems so far away now. I hope my old home, my old money, can make someone else's life as much a dream as my own."

The women sat in silence, each pondering their happy end after varying sadness in beginnings.

"I heard Benedict's brother and family are coming to visit," Mariah asked.

Vivien nodded. "Yes. The dowager, the earl and his wife, as well as their children, will be here at the end of the summer. Over the past year, much of the ice between them has melted. The two women even correspond with me. Ultimately, I believe it will be a very joyful trip."

Lysandra laughed. "Goodness, my dear, it seems after all your hardship, you truly created very happy lives for yourself and for us. What a matchmaker you turned out to be."

Vivien looked at her friends. Lysandra was wrong in some ways. As a mistress matchmaker, she had ultimately failed. But as a match-maker for love and devotion, she was a great success indeed. And as the ocean waves lapped her feet, she congratulated herself one final time and was utterly grateful for the life and love she had accepted and created with the man at her side.

ALSO BY JESS MICHAELS

The Kent's Row Duchesses

No Dukes Allowed

Not Another Duke

Not the Duke You Marry

Theirs

Their Marchioness

Their Duchess

Their Countess

Their Bride (Coming January 2024)

Regency Royals

To Protect a Princess

Earl's Choice

Princes are Wild

To Kiss a King

The Queen's Man

The Three Mrs

The Unexpected Wife

The Defiant Wife

The Duke's Wife

The Duke's By-Blows

The Love of a Libertine

The Heart of a Hellion

The Matter of a Marquess

The Redemption of a Rogue

The 1797 Club

The Daring Duke

Her Favorite Duke

The Broken Duke

The Silent Duke

The Duke of Nothing

The Undercover Duke

The Duke of Hearts

The Duke Who Lied

The Duke of Desire

The Last Duke

The Scandal Sheet

The Return of Lady Jane

Stealing the Duke

Lady No Says Yes

My Fair Viscount

Guarding the Countess

The House of Pleasure

Seasons

An Affair in Winter

A Spring Deception

One Summer of Surrender

Adored in Autumn

The Wicked Woodleys

Forbidden

Deceived

Tempted

Ruined

Seduced

Fascinated

To see a complete listing of Jess Michaels' titles, please visit:

http://www.authorjessmichaels.com/books

ABOUT THE AUTHOR

USA Today Bestselling author Jess Michaels likes geeky stuff, Cherry Vanilla Coke Zero, anything coconut, cheese and her dog, Elton. She is lucky enough to be married to her favorite person in the world and lives in Oregon settled between the ocean and the mountains.

When she's not trying out new flavors of Greek yogurt or rewatching Bob's Burgers over and over and over (she's a Tina), she writes historical romances with smoking hot characters and emotional stories. She has written for numerous publishers and is now fully indie and loving every moment of it (well, almost every moment).

Jess loves to hear from fans! So please feel free to contact her at Jess@AuthorJessMichaels.com.

Jess Michaels offers a free book to members of her newsletter, so sign up on her website:
http://www.AuthorJessMichaels.com/

facebook.com/JessMichaelsBks

instagram.com/JessMichaelsBks

bookbub.com/authors/jess-michaels